BFFs

Play to Win

LATCHMERE SCHOOL
Latchmere Road
Kingston Upon Thames
Surrey KT2 5TT

For Holly – this will be you soon!

STRIPES PUBLISHING
An imprint of Little Tiger Press
1 The Coda Centre, 189 Munster Road,
London SW6 6AW

A paperback original
First published in Great Britain in 2013

Text copyright © Belinda Rapley, 2013

ISBN: 978-1-84715-370-8

The right of Belinda Rapley to be identified
as the author of this work has been asserted by
her in accordance with the Copyright,
Designs and Patents Act, 1988.

Printed and bound in the UK.

10 9 8 7 6 5 4 3 2 1

Holly Robbins

BFFs

Play to Win

stripes

Being a twin spells double trouble for Lexie's birthday plans!

Jas was the last to arrive at Lexie's. She appeared in a whirlwind of excitement, leaping out of her mum's car and flying up the path to the front door. Me, Nisha and Lexie had been sitting in the living room, chatting. It was Friday of the February half-term holiday and Lexie had invited us over to spend the day at her house. It was almost a week since we'd last seen each other – at a sleepover at Nisha's to say goodbye to her step-sister, Poppy, who was finally going home to London.

We rushed into the hallway and Lexie flung open the door.

"I'm back!" Jas cried, a huge grin on her face. "Did

you miss me?!"

"We hardly got a chance to," Lexie joked, as Jas rushed in, "not with all the texts and photos you've been sending!"

"London looked amazing," I smiled, giving Jas a welcome-back hug. Jas and me had been best friends for years, and not seeing her for a week did feel like forever! "Tell us all about it properly!"

We bundled back into the living room.

"Ooh, before I forget," Jas said, pulling an envelope out of her neon-pink handbag. "Poppy gave me this for Luke." She handed the envelope to Lexie. Luke was Lexie's twin brother, and a romance had blossomed between him and Poppy while she'd been staying.

"A love letter!" Nisha said, as Lexie sniffed it.

"It's got perfume on!" Lexie squealed. She stepped out of the room and shouted up the stairs. "Luke!"

"Your bag's so cool, Jas!" I gasped.

"Thanks, Ellie! Poppy helped me choose it," Jas giggled. "Her mum took me, Poppy and Poppy's best friend Angel to Topshop on Oxford Street. You've never seen a shop so huge! It was awesome – the changing rooms there go on forEVER! And there's a café, and a hair salon, and a section full of vintage clothes!"

6

Play to Win

Jas had spent the week visiting her dad, who lived in London. She didn't often go down to see him, so the trip had been a big deal.

At that moment, Luke appeared at the door. He had the same blue eyes and scruffy dark hair as Lexie. He was in a different form at Priory Road, so we didn't see much of him at school. Seeing them at home together was weirdsville. They looked so similar, and they even had the same dress sense – Lexie was happiest wearing her hoody and tracksuit bottoms … and so was Luke!

"What's up?" he asked. "I'm just on my way out to the park for a kickabout."

"Oh, nothing," Jas said casually, before breaking into a grin. "It's only a letter from your girlfriend, that's all…"

Luke couldn't keep the smile off his face. "Thanks, Jas. Poppy mentioned she was sending something back with you."

Jas nodded. "And you don't have to ask – she did go on about you, the whole time!"

Luke grinned. "I, um, better just…"

He took the pale green envelope from Lexie and backed out of the room, then we heard him run upstairs. A couple of minutes later he jumped back down the stairs two at a time, a spring in his step.

"See you later!" he called out. The next second the front door slammed.

"Come on, Jas, tell us more about London!" I said.

"Well, it was awesome spending time with Dad. He took us to the Tate Modern one afternoon, and we went to see a play at Wimbledon theatre, too. That was so much fun, but I kept wishing I was up on the stage rather than sat in the audience! And then there was London Fashion Week. Poppy and Angel wanted us all to go," Jas confessed. "It was on while I was there. So cool! But there was no way we could get tickets. So, we just did our own fashion show … in the Topshop changing rooms!"

Jas had us all giggling as she started to pull model poses.

"Oh, I've got an idea!" Nisha suddenly rummaged in her bag. She pulled out a swish-looking camera.

"Wow!" Lexie gasped. "Is that yours?"

"It was Mum's birthday last Sunday and Dave bought her a new camera. She said I could have her old one."

"That's awesome!" I said, peering over Nisha's shoulder to get a closer look.

Play to Win

"It's like a birthday present without it even being your birthday!" Jas added.

"I know," Nisha smiled, "I feel really lucky. But I haven't had a chance to play around with it yet, so come on – get posing – I need to test it!"

Me, Jas and Lexie looked at each other, then began pulling crazy model faces, following Jas's lead as she strutted back and forth, while Nisha took lots of photos.

"All of you squeeze in!" Nisha giggled. "I'm going to try to set the timer!"

Nisha frowned as she pressed a few buttons. We put our heads close together, grinning for the camera. Well, I say grinning – Jas was grimacing, trying to make us giggle. Nisha balanced the camera on the arm of the sofa and rushed towards us. She dived in front, just as the camera went off.

We were making so much noise that Smarty and Jinx, Lexie's two huge chocolate Labradors, bounded into the room, eager to join in the fun. They danced all round us, barking madly. Smarty licked my face, making me squeal and Nisha caught it all on camera!

Puffed out, we collapsed on to the sofa and looked through Nisha's shots on the viewfinder, which set us off with fresh fits of giggles.

"That was awesome," Jas smiled, flumping back on the cushions.

"It's your birthday soon, isn't it, Lexie?" Nisha asked.

Lexie's face lit up. "Yes! And for the first year ever, me and Luke are allowed to pick what we want to do separately, rather than have a joint party. But guess what?"

"What?"

"We both want to go to The Adventure Forest!" Lexie jokingly groaned.

"You're such a twin," Jas grinned. "You make out that you're so different, but you're totally alike!"

"Not in everything!" Lexie laughed.

"Oh no?" Nisha smiled, nodding at Lexie's clothes. "It's not like you dress the same or anything, is it?"

Lexie grinned. "We never mean to!" she protested. "It must just be a twin thing..."

"Would you prefer to be more different, then?" I asked.

Lexie thought about it for a second, then shook her head. "Well, there are still lots of ways we're different, but I do kind of like being a twin. We look out for each other. And Luke's pretty cool most of the time. Except when he's with his mates, that is. Then he acts like I've got the lurgy! But it can be fun sharing birthdays and stuff. And it'll be fun seeing which of us is better at The Adventure Forest!"

"Um, am I the only one who's never heard of The Adventure Forest?" Nisha asked, looking round.

I shook my head. "I haven't, either."

Lexie raised her eyebrows in disbelief. "Me and Luke haven't been before, but we've wanted to go for ages. We saw it in *Boredom Bashers* on TV!" Lexie said. "It looks so incredible! You get to go up on this trail through the tree tops and swing between the trees on zipwires..."

Lexie leaped off the sofa to demonstrate, making Smarty and Jinx bark excitedly. They dived on Lexie, thinking it was some kind of game. At that moment Mrs Jones came into the room carrying a tray of freshly cooked cupcakes. She put them down on the table.

"Cakes, anyone?" she asked, as Lexie jumped up from the floor. "What are you up to?"

"We're talking about Lexie's birthday plans," Jas said. "Lexie was giving us a demonstration of what we'll be getting up to at The Adventure Forest!"

Lexie's mum gave Lexie a look. "Hold your horses,

Lexie. It's not definitely happening, remember."

Lexie scowled and turned to us abruptly. "Come on, who fancies taking the dogs for a walk?"

She stomped out into the hallway and pulled on her trainers. It wasn't a question – we were going out. Me, Nisha and Jas exchanged glances, then followed Lexie, abandoning the cakes.

Smarty and Jinx jogged eagerly next to Lexie as she marched ahead of us to the park. I raised an eyebrow at Nisha and Jas. They shrugged, like they didn't have a clue what the matter was, either.

"What's up, Lexie? Are you OK?" I said as the three of us hurried forward to catch up with her.

Lexie sighed and didn't say anything at first. We had reached the gates of the park so she let the dogs off their leads. They bounded away, snuffling the bushes, zigzagging along the path ahead of us.

"You know what I just said about liking being a twin?" she said, as we carried on walking. "Well, I take that back. In fact, sometimes I hate it, especially with a brother as swot-tastic as Luke."

I wasn't sure how that had anything to do with The Adventure Forest, but I didn't have to wait long to find out.

Play to Win

"Not only is he great at sports, but he's clever, too!" Lexie went on. "He always does his homework on time, and he comes top in nearly every subject. That's one way we're completely different! Compared to him my marks look terrible. So, Mum and Dad have said I've got to work extra hard and improve my marks this half term or I can't go to The Adventure Forest for my birthday. It really sucks!"

"We can always help with your work," I pointed out, "if you're worried about your marks, I mean."

"I'm just so busy," Lexie explained. "What with team training for netball, plus cross-country running and drama club, I always seem to run out of time for homework!"

Ahead of us to the right of the path was an expanse of flat parkland where everyone played football. Luke and a group of other boys from our year at Priory Road were kicking a ball around. Lexie watched, following the action as Max expertly dribbled the ball past Jordan. Damon sprinted forward and performed a sliding tackle. He managed to tap the ball away from Max, amidst loud protests from some of the other boys that he'd fouled.

Jas rubbed her hands together. The sun was pale in

the cloudless sky and there was a chill in the air. "Does anyone fancy a hot chocolate?"

Lexie reluctantly turned away from the game and we headed to the little park café. We took our steaming hot chocolates back outside and sat on the bench, facing the game. Luke had the ball and was sprinting down the field, tapping it ahead of him. Darren dived and just got a hand to it, deflecting it straight at us! It rolled along the ground and came to a stop, right by my feet.

"Hey! Can you kick it back?" Max shouted. The boys all stood on the pitch, looking over.

"There's no way I'm touching it!" I squeaked, feeling my cheeks burn red. "You do it, Lexie!"

Smarty, who'd trotted back to the bench, barked and sniffed the ball. Lexie put down her hot chocolate and jumped up, hooking the ball over towards her with her foot.

Luke waved to her. "Pass it here, Lex," he shouted.

Lexie looked over to him, took aim, and hoofed it back to him so it landed right ahead of him and rolled to a stop at his feet.

"That was a decent shot!" Darren said, sounding surprised.

14

Play to Win

Lexie grinned. "It should be – I play with Luke and Dad all the time."

"I bet she manages to get past you, too, Luke!" Sam beamed, cuffing Luke round the head. The others broke into laughter.

"No chance," Luke said, looking embarrassed. "Get lost, Lex. We're trying to have a serious game here, I don't need my sister hanging around."

Lexie shrugged her shoulders, sat back down on the bench and picked up her cup.

"That was awesome!" I said, taking a gulp of my hot chocolate before it got too cold. "You're ace at football, Lexie! I didn't realize."

"I really love it," Lexie said. "Not that I get that much chance to play – Luke and his mates hate me butting in on their games."

"They just don't want to get shown up by a girl." Jas nudged Lexie. "That's all."

Lexie smiled. "Maybe."

We sat looking at the boys carrying on with their kickabout.

"Is anyone else cold?" I asked. The blasts of wind whipped straight through my jacket.

"A bit," Nisha agreed. "Shall we head back?"

Lexie called the two dogs and clipped their leads back on, then we wandered towards the park gates. "I've got loads to do when I get home," Lexie grumbled. "I haven't even started my half-term holiday homework yet."

Jas's eyebrows shot skywards. "Er, what was all that about trying extra hard?" she said, nudging Lexie with a grin.

Lexie laughed groaningly. "I know! Ugh, I'm so not looking forward to the next six weeks. Like, at all!"

A new idea at Priory Road leads to a pact between me and my BFFs!

It was Monday morning, the first day of a new half term at Priory Road. Jas and I always got the bus together, and we had arranged to meet Lexie and Nisha outside the gates, which had become our tradition on the first day of school. Although I wasn't over the moon to be back, I did feel really at home among the crowds of students mingling around the entrance. Kirsty, self-proclaimed Queen Bee of our form, glided by with her best friend, Eliza. They ignored everyone as usual, with their button noses in the air.

"Luke has been chatting to Poppy loads," Lexie said. "They've been on the phone, and messaging non-stop.

I chatted to her last night, too – it was way more interesting than my history homework, which I kind of forgot about. Oops!"

"Hmm, I can't see Mr Wood accepting that as an excuse," Jas said with a smile, as we walked through the double doors into school. Jas was right – our history teacher was fearsome, and very particular about homework. "I can hear him now," Jas went on, as we headed for the lockers. "'Miss Jones, you take responsibility for your own learning! This modern-day technology is far too distracting! Detention, my office!'"

We all giggled at Jas putting on a deep voice and imitating Mr Wood.

Suddenly Lexie's face lit up. "Oooh, look who's arrived!" she whispered, nudging me. I turned to see Ed and Zac heading for the lockers, right where we were standing.

"It's your boyfriend, Ellie!" Jas whispered loudly.

"Jas!" I said, thwacking her. "He is so not my boyfriend!" Even so, Jas's comments had made me turn completely scarlet.

Last term Ed had sent me my very first Valentine card. He'd been about to ask me to dance at the

Play to Win

Valentine's disco, too – at least that's what Jas reckoned. Only we'd all dodged off to the loos before he got a chance! My BFFs hadn't let me forget it ever since.

"Hey – Woody! What's so funny?" Ed asked, seeing us all glancing over and giggling.

"I was just saying…" Jas started, but I managed to pinch her arm. She collapsed into giggles again!

"Girls," Zac said, shaking his head as he passed us. "They're just weird."

"Tell me about it," Ed said. But he caught my eye and smiled. I bit my lip, trying to stop myself from smiling back.

"He so fancies you!" Lexie gasped.

"But does Ellie like Ed…?" Nisha said teasingly.

My cheeks went all hot for a second, and I turned to my locker quickly.

"As if!" I replied, my face hidden. I rummaged about a bit, even though I had all the books I needed in my bag already. "Anyway, can we please drop the whole Ed thing now?" I asked, closing my locker. I did my best Kirsty impression. "It's *so* last half term."

"You sounded just like Frosty Face then!" Lexie laughed.

We called Kirsty "Frosty Face" because she hardly ever smiled – she was always too busy trying to look sophisticated and avoiding wrinkles.

The bell rang and we dashed off to our form room for registration, arriving moments before Miss Dubois, our form teacher. It took her ages to get us settled – the classroom was buzzing with everyone swapping stories about their half-term holidays.

"*Maintenant*, I have something exciting to tell you. We have a special week to start this half term," Miss Dubois announced, as everyone finally stopped talking. "It's called 'Inspiration Week'. For this we will have a special guest joining us every morning. There will be all-school assemblies and some of the lessons you'll have will tie in with the Inspiration Week theme – it's our first year doing this; all of the teachers hope it will be fun!"

A murmur rose, as everyone whispered to each other.

"Imagine if a popstar strolled into assembly?!" Jas gasped, turning to me.

"Do you reckon?" I asked, unconvinced. This was Priory Road after all, not a talent school.

Miss Dubois smiled, then announced who was

coming in. She mentioned a scientist, an author, an explorer and a journalist, then she told us who was visiting first.

"Today, after registration, Demba Keshi will be coming in."

"Er, who?" Ed asked.

"Only the best footballer, ever!" Lexie gasped. "He plays for our Championship side in the football league!"

Most of the boys were football-mad. They looked part shocked, part mega-excited, and everyone started talking at once.

Even Kirsty was impressed. "I'm his biggest fan, seriously!" She swooned, fanning herself with her hand. "That's amazing!"

"And one more thing, before we go to assembly. We will be having a parents' evening this half term," Miss Dubois announced, earning a collective groan from the class. I felt a tingle of nervousness. Miss Dubois started to pass round a stack of letters. "These are for your parents. I need them back by the end of next week. Your parents will automatically be given appointments to see me and teachers for your core subjects, but they are to tick which other subject teachers they wish to see. *Oui?*"

"D'you reckon I could get away with just chucking this in the bin?" Ed whispered as Miss Dubois handed round the letters. "Then my parents wouldn't have to listen to all the teachers telling them how amazing I am. Amazingly bad, that is!"

"I wish I could get rid of mine, too!" Lexie sighed.

The bell went and we all rushed to the door, despite Miss Dubois's calls for us to slow down. Lexie was leading the way, jostling for position with all the boys.

Demba Keshi was wearing a sharp, tight-fitting dark grey suit. As he spoke softly into the microphone you could have heard a pin drop. I stole a quick glance round – nearly the whole school was enthralled. He was a celebrity, standing right there, on our stage!

It was really interesting to hear about his life, and how he had got into playing professional football. He talked about how hard the team trained and what they did in preparation for a match. But after twenty minutes of non-stop football talk, there were a few shuffles in the hall. Jas leaned against me, and gave a mock yawn, making me giggle.

Play to Win

Once he had finished speaking we were allowed to ask questions. I looked round to see who was brave enough. A whole load of hands shot up. Jordan, captain of the Year Seven football team, got the final question and asked what Demba's top tips were for being the best.

"I've only got two tips," Demba said. "But they're big ones. The first is – follow your dreams. It's true, not everyone gets to fulfil them. But, if you don't try, you'll never find out if you could have done. The second? Practice. No one gets very far without practising, even those with the most talent. As long as you're the best you can be, you've done all you can."

"I think they're valuable lessons we should all learn." Our headmaster, Mr Langdell, beamed. "What a wonderful way to begin Inspiration Week. Now, can everyone put their hands together to show our appreciation for Demba Keshi!"

We had double PE first thing on Monday and Lexie looked fired up by the talk. She flashed round the netball court, dodging past defenders, shooting and scoring from miles out – I felt dizzy just watching her! After being singled out for praise by Terrifying Townsend, our super-scary PE teacher, Lexie took a deep breath. "I will get to The Adventure Forest for my birthday," she said, sounding determined. "I just need to work really, really hard in lessons!"

"Demba Keshi would be proud," Nisha grinned. "You've got to follow your dream to get to The Adventure Forest!"

I'm not into football, but Demba's talk had been pretty awesome. "I reckon we should make a pact," I said, looking round at my BFFs. "We should all follow our dreams, whatever they are."

"Too right!" Jas added. Then she grinned. "I'm so glad Demba came to speak to us today."

"Really?" I asked, suspicious. Jas had a wicked look in her eye. She had never shown any interest in football before, ever.

"Yup," she giggled. "I've wanted to go to The Adventure Forest for ages. Now Demba's inspired you, Lexie, I might just get there!"

We have to work on a kidnap case (seriously!) and Lexie gets in a spin...

The next morning a forensic scientist, Eve Scardino, was our guest speaker in assembly. She told us about her job working with detectives. She made everybody squirm by talking about how she had to study maggots. Forensic scientists are involved in murder investigations, and Eve said that if someone's been dead for a while, there'll be maggots. If you can age the maggots, then you know how long the person's been dead for.

"Clever stuff, right?" Eve asked, smiling round at everyone.

"Eww, gross, more like!" Kirsty squealed. For once,

25

I had to agree with her. That was one job I would never want to do!

The only person who didn't seem freaked out by it was Ajay. He's so into science, and he looked as in love with Eve as Kirsty had been with Demba Keshi.

We had chemistry after assembly on Tuesday, and Eve had put together a crime scene investigation for us. Taped to the whiteboard was a poster with a picture of our headmaster. Underneath was one word: Kidnapped! There were three suspects and we had to work out which one had written the ransom note and link them to the clothes fibres and fingerprints at the scene.

"Come and collect your instructions and equipment from the front," Miss Dale said over the hubbub. "You can work in teams of four."

Me, Jas, Lexie and Nisha all grinned at each other and went up to get everything we needed. We quickly read through the instructions and then started setting up the microscope. Lexie was looking at the instructions closely, reading them through.

"OK, are we set?" Nisha asked, as we all stood about in our white coats, putting on our goggles. Me and Jas nodded.

"I think so," Lexie frowned.

"Shall we take a task each?" Nisha suggested.

"But then we won't all know how to do it," Lexie said. "I think we should stick together for all of it."

"Um, OK," we agreed. "Right, let's start with the fibres. Three of us can prepare the slides, and the fourth person can look at them under the microscope."

Lexie took charge of the microscope and we passed her the slides when they were ready. Lexie slipped the first one under the lens, leaned forward, and looked down the eyepiece.

"I need to magnify it," she muttered to herself. She took hold of the knob on the side of the microscope, and turned it. Only she turned it the wrong way.

"Not that way!" Jas squeaked, just as the lens scrunched down on the slide, completely wrecking it. "It says to turn it to the left!"

"Sorry!" Lexie said, looking flustered and reading the instructions again. She cleared away the slide as Jas made up a new one. "Maybe I should write everything up, instead, while you three do the experiments?"

Jas looked crestfallen. "I didn't mean for you to not be in charge of the microscope, Lexie."

"You've still got to be part of the experiment," I added, trying to make Lexie feel better.

"Well, I will be if I'm writing it up, won't I?" Lexie said snappily. Me, Jas and Nisha exchanged a surprised glance, then got on with the work. Lexie watched and made notes while me, Jas and Nisha worked through the experiments, ruling out each suspect one by one until we were left with the guilty one – our fierce history teacher and deputy head, Mr Wood!

"I knew it would be him!" Jas giggled.

"So, hang on," Lexie frowned, looking at her notes, "how come you ruled out Mr Flight?"

At that moment, Miss Dale called for us to tidy away so we could go through our results before the end of the lesson. Miss Dale chose one group to explain how they had reached their conclusion.

"Does everyone understand?" Miss Dale smiled round the room. I noticed that Lexie was still looking through the notes. "Lexie?"

"Yes," she said quickly. "All clear, thanks, miss."

Our homework was to write up our notes and take our own fingerprints.

As we walked over to our next lesson, Nisha said, "I wouldn't mind being a forensic scientist. I'm not sure about the grisly murder scenes, though!"

"I know what you mean!" Jas agreed.

"I could never be a scientist," I said. "All that deduction and analysis! It's mind-boggling. How about you, Lexie?" I asked.

Lexie was trailing behind us, keeping quiet. She looked up when I said her name, and smiled, but it was clear that she hadn't been listening to the conversation.

In fact, she didn't say much for the rest of the morning and then at lunch she went off to cross-country practice.

Nisha turned to me and Jas. "Do you fancy coming with me to find out more about the photography club? I'm really getting into taking photos with Mum's old camera!"

"Course!" Jas grinned. We headed off to the Social noticeboard. There was a whole section dedicated to the photography club, with a montage of photos taken by members of the club.

"Wow, they're pretty impressive," I said as Nisha studied them closely. "And look, it says 'new members welcome'!"

Nisha grinned, getting excited. "They meet every

Wednesday after school." She made a note in her diary of the room number and time. "I can't wait!"

The first lesson in the afternoon was PSHE. Our teacher, Mr Blaxhall, announced that we would be developing a project over the course of that half term, linked to Inspiration Week.

"I want you all to come up with a campaign for change," he announced. "Think of something you feel passionately about – it can be something you want to introduce at school, or in the community, or something you think should be done differently. You'll need to design a poster, prepare a five-minute talk to persuade your classmates and develop a storyboard for a TV advert. I'd like you to spend this lesson coming up with your campaign topic."

"Can it be about anything?" Kirsty asked.

Mr Blaxhall nodded. "Anything, as long as it fits into the criteria for creating change."

"I know what I'm going to campaign for," Kirsty said smugly, opening her notebook. "I think that Priory Road should introduce a GCSE in modelling!"

Jas rolled her eyes.

Play to Win

"Feel free to form groups, so that you can discuss your ideas," Mr Blaxhall added.

Lexie and Nisha turned their chairs to face us and the whole class began to chatter and swap ideas for the project.

"I know," Jas suddenly piped up. "I wish that this school did more creative stuff, like circus skills, or dance. I'd love that!"

"That's a great idea!" I said.

But the rest of us were struggling to come up with anything and Lexie resorted to doodling over her notebook. Finally I got an idea and just as I opened my mouth to tell the others, Nisha clapped her hands, her face lighting up. We laughed. "You first!" I said.

"I was just thinking that it would be amazing to have a nature trail in the woods near my house!" Nisha said. "It could teach you all about the wildlife and it could even have arty things in it – like sculptures made from natural materials. How cool would that be! What was your idea, Ellie?"

"I was thinking about a school newspaper," I said, getting even more excited as I started to talk about it. "It could have stories and articles contributed by the students."

Mr Blaxhall appeared behind us and leaned over. "That's a very interesting idea, Ellie." My face flushed. "How about you three?"

Jas and Nisha told Mr Blaxhall their ideas. He asked them a few questions, then he turned to Lexie. "How about you, Lexie? What do you want to change?"

Lexie shook her head. "Um, I haven't really come up with anything yet…"

"Well, why don't you try brainstorming? Make a note of everything that pops into your head – I'm sure you'll hit upon an idea you like."

Near the end of the lesson Mr Blaxhall asked for some people to share their ideas with the whole class. Ed put his hand up first. He had come up with a campaign to revamp the local skateboarding park. It was so rundown that some of the older ramps weren't even safe to use any more.

"That's actually quite sensible," I whispered to Jas, surprised.

"Maybe there's more to Ed than meets the eye," Jas nodded in agreement.

Trin wanted to introduce advanced learning groups at school, while Zophia went for something huge – she wanted the Polish community to be more accepted locally, starting with introducing a Polish café that held events so that everyone could learn more about the culture.

The minute the bell rang, Lexie started shoving her books in her bag. She was keeping her head down, but I noticed that her eyes were welling up with tears.

"Lexie, are you OK?" I asked.

She tried to brush it off. "I'm fine. I just can't think of any good ideas, that's all. I'm never going to get to The Adventure Forest at this rate!"

A tear rolled down her cheek.

"We'll all help you, won't we?" Nisha said quickly. Me and Jas nodded and huddled round her, so the others wouldn't see she was crying.

"Course we will," Jas agreed, giving Lexie a quick hug.

"We'll come up with an idea between us by Friday, promise," I said.

Lexie looked at us gratefully, and smiled a wobbly smile.

Jas sets her sights on stardom and a football kickstarts Lexie's project!

"Everyone, I want you to give a special welcome to our guest tonight as part of Inspiration Week," Mrs Crawfield announced in drama club that evening. The side door of the hall opened and in walked a young woman with glossy black hair and huge blue eyes!

"I'm sure you all recognize her as the presenter of *Boredom Bashers* on television." Mrs Crawfield beamed. "Saffy Fine!"

"Hi, guys!" Saffy grinned. "It's great to join you all tonight – especially as my career in television started in an after-school drama club, just like this one!"

Jas looked like she needed the loo she was so excited.

Play to Win

Saffy told us all about what life was like behind the scenes on a television set, and about how much time and work goes into just a few minutes on air. She talked about how scary it was the first time she had to do a live show and she told us about some bloopers, too.

"And Saffy's not just here to talk," Mrs Crawfield added. "She's going to help us with some drama exercises that would be useful for television work, too! Saffy – over to you!"

"Right, for our first exercise, I think we should have you all preparing for a piece direct to camera!" Saffy said. Jas took it really seriously, hanging on Saffy's every word. We paired up, ready to start, before Saffy counted us down to "going live"! This was going to be the best drama club ever!

The hour raced by. We packed loads in, but it seemed like only five minutes had passed when Mrs Crawfield called the end of the club. Saffy asked if anyone had any last questions before she left. Jas asked if Saffy could tell her what the most useful bit of training for a job in television was.

"As well as doing a drama club like this one," Saffy said, "I also did a performing arts class on Saturdays –

we did singing, circus skills, comedy – loads of stuff! That really helped prepare me."

"That is so what I want to do!" Jas squeaked as we headed to the cloakrooms. "I just need to persuade Mum to let me – it's vital for my future career as a super-famous TV presenter!"

Wednesday's Inspiration Week speaker was an explorer who had been to the North and South Poles. He told us all about his close encounters with polar bears and made us think about geography in a totally different way to our dull teacher, Mr "Wiggy" Wigglesworth.

"I wonder if Wiggy will be inspired by the talk?" Lexie joked as we headed to geography. "Inspired to give us a good geography lesson!"

But Mr "Wiggy" Wigglesworth was as dull as ever.

"He must have been asleep during that assembly!" Jas groaned.

In history, at least, Mr Wood managed to capture some of the excitement. We talked about Captain Scott and his trip to the Antarctic. But Lexie sat quietly, and didn't get involved. I'd heard Mr Wood ask to see her at the end of the lesson as he'd handed our homework back. I hoped she wasn't in trouble – she was having enough hassle with her work already.

When the bell rang, Lexie went reluctantly to the front of the class. Me, Jas and Nisha hung about in the corridor, waiting for her. Lexie slunk out a few minutes later.

"So, what did he want?" Jas asked.

Lexie grimaced. "He wanted to know if I'd understood the homework, that was all."

"And did you?" Nisha asked.

"Course I did!" Lexie said, making a face. "I just didn't have time to answer the questions fully."

Mr Wood appeared behind us. "Off you go," he said, and we hurried off down the corridor.

The next morning, Nisha was eager to fill us in on her first photography club meeting from the night before.

"Everyone was so friendly and I picked up loads of tips! They run a competition each term, too. This time the subject's 'Springtime'."

"Are you going to enter?" Lexie asked.

Nisha nodded. "I've got loads of ideas already!"

"That's great," Jas grinned.

"Come on!" I said. "I want to get to assembly. I'm really interested to hear what this reporter's got to say."

We reached the hall and filed in. Jim Fazakerly, the chief reporter from our local newspaper, had loads of stories about people he'd interviewed and events he'd covered. Some of them were serious, but there were some funny ones, too – one was about a café just for dogs!

"I'd so love to be a journalist!" I said as we headed to our first lesson. "I can't wait to get going on my school newspaper project. I've started to write some articles – I thought I could make one to hand round while I give my talk!"

Lexie groaned. "Our next PSHE lesson's tomorrow and I still haven't got a clue what to do for my project!"

"Sorry, Lexie," I said, suddenly feeling guilty. "I didn't mean to go on about it."

"I just wish I had something to get excited about, the way you three do," Lexie said.

All through the day we tried to come up with ideas for Lexie, but none of them sparked her imagination.

Play to Win

By Friday lunch, time was running out. We headed out into the playground after we'd eaten. Jas's brother Josh was kicking a ball around with some of the other Year Nine boys. We weren't really paying them any attention, but then a ball came flying in our direction and Lexie instinctively stopped it with the inside of her shin, getting it under control. She trapped it under her foot and looked over to where the boys were playing. Lexie's eyes lit up as she decided who to pass it back to. She booted the ball right to Josh's feet.

"Nice pass, Lexie!" Josh called out. "The Year Seven team could use a player like you!" He turned and the boys carried on playing.

"Fat chance of that," Lexie muttered, "when girls don't even get to play football at Priory Road."

Jas gasped and grabbed Lexie's arm. "That's it!"

"What is?" asked Lexie.

"Your project! You should campaign to get a girls' football team at Priory Road!" Jas cried.

Lexie's face broke into the most enormous grin. "Jas, you're a legend – why didn't I think of that?!"

At that moment the bell went.

"Come on, what are you all waiting for, there's a

lesson to get to!" Lexie giggled, racing ahead of us.

Lexie filled page after page of notes during the class.

"Look, there's almost smoke coming off her pen!" I smiled, nudging Jas. "I've never seen you write so fast, Lexie!"

Lexie looked up and grinned, then got back to her work. Me and Jas exchanged a surprised smile. Clearly nothing was going to distract Lexie from her new project!

At the end of the day we grabbed the books we needed for homework from our lockers.

"Ugh, I can't believe Mr Zyal's set us so many algebra questions," I groaned, pulling out my maths textbook. "They're my worst nightmare."

"Mine, too," Lexie said. "It's going to take me ages to get them all done. And I want to get on with my project! OMG – did you hear what I just said? I actually want to do some homework – I must have a fever!"

We all giggled. Lexie and homework never really went together. Maybe the promise of The Adventure Forest was starting to take effect!

"I know!" I said. "Why don't you all come over to mine tomorrow? We could have a homework sleepover to work on our projects together! I'll need to check with Mum and Dad first, though."

"A homework sleepover?" Jas said, sounding unsure. "Well, I guess if anything could make it more bearable, that might be it!"

"I'll text you all when I get home to say for definite," I said.

I had to scoot to catch the bus, so that I could have something to eat at home before swimming practice. As soon as I got back, I asked Mum breathlessly about the sleepover. She was as surprised as Jas to begin with.

"Well, that's a new one on me," she smiled, "but it sounds good!"

"Thanks, Mum!"

As I shovelled in my jacket potato with a fork in one hand, I texted quickly with the other.

All ok – come round early, then we'll have loads of time! xx

I heard a car door slam and a key in the front door. Dad strode in, ruffled my hair and kissed Mum. As I finished dinner and headed off to swimming with him, I felt really excited about the sleepover plan! It was the first time my BFFs would be coming over for a sleepover, and even though we had homework planned for the main event, I was going to make sure it was fun!

5

Shhh! Keep it secret – we're holding a homework club at my house!

"Mum, is there another sleeping bag?" I called down the stairs. I was feeling quite nervous – even though Jas had stayed over at my house a billion times, I really wanted Nisha and Lexie to like it! Crumble padded about between the piles of bedding I'd dumped in the middle of my bedroom floor. The rest of my room was a mess of books and clothes. Crumble purred, butting my leg and then rolling over, wanting his tummy tickled. "Not now, Crumble!" I giggled, "I've got to sort this lot out before everyone gets here – you're not helping!"

I scooped him up and laid him on the bed, tickling

under his rumbling chin. Mum appeared at the door, a sleeping bag and blanket over her arm. "Here you go." She smiled, looking round. "Want a hand sorting this lot out?"

I made a face. "Yes, please!"

Between us it didn't take long to tidy everything up. Then we laid out the sleeping bags, pillows and blankets.

"Perfect!" I cheered.

Dad was in the hall when we headed back downstairs. "I've tidied all my mess up from the table, ready for your homework club," he winked.

"It's not an actual club, Dad," I said, rolling my eyes. "It's just a one-off to work on our projects, that's all."

The doorbell rang. Even without opening the door I knew who was behind it – I could see the outline of Jas's ringletted hair through the frosted glass.

"First one here!" Dad grinned as he opened the door.

"Course!" Jas smiled back. "Got to pick the best bed before Nisha and Lexie get here!"

Me and Jas raced upstairs. Jas bagsied which spot she was sleeping in and then the doorbell rang again and we heard Mum opening it.

Play to Win

"They're upstairs," Mum said. There was thudding, then the bedroom door was flung open and Nisha and Lexie came in together.

"Hey, Ellie," Nisha beamed. "Hi, Jas."

"This is such a nice room, Ellie," Lexie said. "I love all your posters!" She slung her bag down. "Right, so, are we working up here?"

"Steady on, Lexie!" Jas giggled.

"I thought we could work on the big table downstairs," I suggested.

"Good idea! I need something to lean on, so my writing won't be a complete mess!" Jas said.

We all grabbed our stuff and went downstairs to set up.

"I've had a trillion ideas about this project already," Lexie said as she spread her notes out around her. "I could hardly sleep last night – how mad's that!"

"Hmm, I haven't been getting that excited," Jas giggled as we got settled, "but I reckon this is the best project we've been given so far at Priory."

"By miles," Lexie added.

Nisha carefully got out her step-dad's laptop and turned it on.

"I've researched some articles about how to set up

nature trails on the internet," she explained as the laptop whirred into life, "and I've downloaded a map of the woodland near my house. I thought I could take some photos of the walk to hand round during the talk."

"Sounds like a fab idea!" I nodded. "Do you think you could take some photos for my mocked-up newspaper, too? That would really bring it to life."

"Course!" Nisha grinned. "I need the practice!"

Lexie looked at all her notes. "I've got so much stuff, I don't know where to start!"

"Why don't you try putting them into piles?" Nisha suggested.

"Or you could borrow my highlighters," I said. "Then you could colour-code bits for your talk, the poster and the advert."

"I could try, I guess..." Lexie said, "although all my ideas have kind of jumbled into one."

We got Lexie to explain them to us and as she did, she was able to group them together. For her poster, she had come up with a slogan – "Girls! Ever fancied football more than a football hottie? If so, Priory Road's all-new, all-girl football team is for YOU!"

"Well, with that headline, you can guarantee one

thing," Jas smiled.

"What's that?" Lexie frow

"Kirsty won't be signing up.

anything more than a football hottie!

We all giggled. Kirsty had had her eye on

Nine football team ever since we started Year Seven

Priory Road in September.

We all got down to planning our campaigns. As I thought about presenting my talk, butterflies flipped in my tummy. If it was like this now, what would it be like on the day?

"The thought of standing up in front of our whole class," I groaned, "is the scariest thing ever!"

"Scary?" Jas said. "We'll be cheering you on – you'll be fine! I can't wait to get up there. I might even demonstrate a few moves!"

Jas grabbed three highlighters from the table and started to juggle with them. She threw them into the air, but only managed to catch one. The other two clattered on to the table.

We laughed as Jas showcased another couple of "moves" she'd been thinking of. Then we got down to concentrating on our ideas. The time went quickly, and it was only when the smell of homemade chilli con carne

...ed to waft from the kitchen that we finally started ...slow down.

"I've managed to get loads done," I said, stretching in my chair.

"Me, too," Nisha agreed.

Lexie grinned. "I've managed to pretty much design my poster," she said, "and I've got a plan for the advert storyboard, too. It'd be so much better if I could actually shoot it... How cool would that be?"

Nisha's eyes lit up. "My camera has a video function, Lexie," she said. "So maybe we could make the advert!"

"I could be the presenter!" Jas volunteered.

"And I'll report on it for my newspaper! It could be my lead article: 'New girls' football team outstrips boys at Priory Road!'"

"It'll be so much fun," Nisha said, beaming, just as the living-room door opened.

"Time for dinner!" Mum said. "Can you clear the table?"

"I brought a DVD for later," Lexie said as we tidied our things away. "It's *Bend It Like Beckham* – it's about girls playing football. I thought it might help inspire me!"

"You don't need any inspiration by the look of

things today!" Nisha said.

After dinner we changed into our PJs so we could get comfy watching the DVD. Jas had a fluffy onesie that she'd bought in London with Poppy and she nearly slipped down the stairs because the feet were so padded! Dad made us hot chocolates as we snuggled down to watch the film.

"So, at least we've made some progress with our PSHE work," Nisha said as we got settled. "Now we've just got maths, history and biology to crack tomorrow!"

Lexie let out a pretend snore, making us giggle. "If it was all as exciting as PSHE I wouldn't mind," she said. "But somehow I don't think that tomorrow's going to be quite so much fun..."

"Just keep thinking of The Adventure Forest," Jas reminded her. "All this hard work will be worth it when you're hurtling through the trees on a zipwire!"

"True," Lexie said, and I could hear the smile in her voice. "That almost makes me want to do it, I guess!"

A mew near my ear woke me up the next morning. "Crumble, shhh!" I whispered croakily. I opened one eye and saw Nisha turn over. She smiled, then sat up.

"What time is it?" she asked.

I checked my alarm clock. "Nearly eight," I said quietly.

Nisha scooped up Crumble and we crept downstairs, leaving the other two still sleeping. Crumble rubbed round us excitedly while we got him some food. As he tucked in we got ourselves some cereal.

Mum was in the kitchen, too, making coffee.

"Do you reckon Lexie's parents will let her go to The Adventure Forest for her birthday?" I asked Nisha.

She sighed. "I don't know. I mean, you'd think she'd be trying really hard right now, but she always seems to have an excuse ready for why she hasn't done her homework. It'll be such a shame if Luke gets to go and she doesn't."

"What do you think, Mum?" I asked.

Mum thought for a second. "I think some twins love being exactly the same as each other, but some want to be as separate as possible. That might be why Lexie doesn't put much effort into her schoolwork, so that she's different to Luke. Or it might be that she finds schoolwork quite difficult but doesn't want to admit it because everyone compares her to Luke. Sometimes it's easier to let everyone think you don't care."

"Really?" I frowned. Lexie had always had a "don't care" attitude towards schoolwork, but I'd never really thought about why before. Maybe Mum had a point.

We heard voices upstairs so we changed the subject. A couple of minutes later Jas and Lexie appeared and, after they had their breakfasts, we got showered and dressed, ready for the next round of homework.

"Should we start with maths?" Nisha asked, grimacing. "Then we get the worst out of the way first."

"Good plan," Jas agreed.

I looked at the letters and numbers all mixed in together on our algebra homework sheets. None of us really understood them that well, but we sweated through them slowly together, pitching in our thoughts. Lexie sat quietly, writing down and rubbing out as we worked out the answers.

As we finished the last one, Jas yippee'd and we thankfully put our maths books away.

"History next!" I smiled, trying to keep the mood upbeat. As we scanned through the questions Mr Wood had set us, Lexie scratched her head, frowning.

History was one of my favourite subjects. I loved it when Mr Wood set really hard questions, but I wondered if, for Lexie, they might be as incomprehensible as I found Mr Zyal's algebra. She reached to the floor and picked up her project notes again. "I don't think I can concentrate on anything else while I've got this project on the go," she said. She shoved her other books out of the way and began adding to her poster design. There was something defiant about the way Lexie did it. I was about to say something, but I bit my tongue. The last thing I wanted to do was end up upsetting my BFF, when we were trying to help her.

"Do you think anything will happen with our projects once we've finished them?" Lexie asked.

"What do you mean?" Jas asked.

"This project's really good fun," Lexie explained, "but it's made me realize how much I really want to get a girls' football team set up at Priory Road! Next to all these stupid history questions, this feels like it means something."

"I don't reckon I'll manage to get clowning skills past the teachers, do you?" Jas giggled. "I've asked Mum about going on a performing arts course, but she said it's too expensive, so I guess I'll just have to stick with drama club."

"That's a shame," Nisha sympathized.

"I'm with Lexie," I said. I'd come up with loads of ideas for articles and interviews. "I'd love to start up a school newspaper, if I could."

"You should go for it, Els! Remember our pact to follow our dreams!" Jas said, just as the doorbell rang. Dad answered it and we heard Dave, Nisha's step-dad say hello.

"We haven't even packed up our stuff!" Nisha panicked. "This morning's flown by!"

Lexie checked her watch. "Perfect," she said, breaking into a grin. "I'll be back just in time for a kickaround with Dad and Luke!"

My homework club might have been fun, but it hadn't helped Lexie the way I'd hoped it might.

Lexie and Nisha left, but Jas stayed at my house a bit longer. We lounged about on the sofa, chatting, until we were interrupted by Jas's phone buzzing with a text.

Just made yoghurt cake – does anyone fancy a warm slice? Mum x

We both jumped off the sofa. Gloria's cakes were epic. I checked with Mum and Dad, then we rushed round.

"Hello!" Jas and I shouted as we burst through the door. Gloria called back to us from the kitchen. She was sitting at the table with Josh and Lulu. The smell of freshly baked cake filled the flat.

"Mmm – this is DE-lish!" Jas said as we tucked in eagerly.

"Fab-u-lous!" I grinned.

"This is what Sunday mornings are all about," Josh sighed, leaning back in his chair and closing his eyes.

Gloria smiled and fed some cake to Lulu, Jas's adorable little sister. We were just debating having a second slice when the phone rang. Gloria and Josh shared a knowing smile.

"I think you better get that, sis," Josh smirked.

"Er, I'm eating!" Jas argued.

"Just do what your brother says," Gloria giggled, nudging Jas towards the phone. Jas rolled her eyes, then stomped into the hall. It wasn't long before we heard a squeal of excitement, then she leaped back into the room.

"Who was it?" I asked. It was clear that Josh and

Play to Win

Gloria already knew.

"Dad!" Jas beamed. She hugged her mum. "He said that you sent the school production of *Oliver!* to him on DVD. He thought I was awesome, obviously … joke! Anyway, he's offered to pay for me to do the performing arts class! Move over, Saffy Fine – Jas Cole has arrived!"

Josh shook his head as Jas danced around the kitchen, a huge beam on her face.

"Jas, that's amazing!" I jumped up and gave her a hug. "I'm so happy for you!"

"Me, too!" Jas giggled, doing a little jig. "It starts next Sunday! How am I supposed to wait till then?"

6

Lexie turns up the heat in our chemistry lesson!

"Has anyone else got their parents' evening appointment letters to return to me?" Miss Dubois stood at the front of the class, her soft brown curls falling down to her shoulders. She tapped the desk with her pen, looking round as Tom and Zac dug about in their bags. Lexie handed hers in, reluctantly.

Miss Dubois took the register, then the bell rang and we headed to PE. We were halfway down the corridor when Jas spotted Mr Blaxhall.

"Quick, Lexie – here's your chance!" Jas said, elbowing her. "Why don't you ask Mr Blaxhall right now about what's going to happen with the PSHE projects once we've finished!"

"Perfect!" Lexie took off at a sprint, dodging round all the bodies in the corridor ahead of her.

We caught up with her just as Mr Blaxhall was giving his verdict. "This is only a project," he pointed out, "but if it has inspired you to actually go out and change something, I'd say go for it. It's worth a try, for sure."

Mr Blaxhall smiled, then swept off up the corridor, saying, "Don't be late for your next lesson!"

"What are you going to do?" Nisha asked. But the fire in Lexie's eyes answered that before she spoke a word.

"We're going to have a girls' football team here at Priory Road – for real, not just for the project! Just wait and see…"

Every time Lexie tried to speak to Terrifying Townsend during PE, she was growled at for interrupting. In the end, Lexie had to wait until the lesson finished. She hurriedly pulled her school uniform back on and raced to Terrifying Townsend's office. Me, Jas and Nisha followed her, but hung back a few steps, peeping round the door.

"Um, Mrs Townsend," Lexie said, as boldly as she

dared, knocking lightly on our teacher's office door.

"What?" she barked.

"I wanted to ask you about starting up a Year Seven girls' football team," Lexie said, a little more uncertainly.

I expected Terrifying Townsend to blast Lexie out of the office for being cheeky or something, but she didn't. She looked like she was chewing over Lexie's idea.

"I've thought about this before," Terrifying Townsend said slowly, "but there wasn't enough interest at the time."

We could see Lexie's shoulders droop.

Terrifying Townsend continued. "But things may have changed and I'd be willing to give it another go," she said. "If you get some interest, I'll hold a taster session. If enough people come to that, I'll consider starting a team."

"For real?" Lexie grinned. A flicker of a smile actually played on Terrifying Townsend's thin lips.

"For real," she nodded.

Lexie whooped and dashed out of Terrifying Townsend's office.

"Did you hear that?" she squealed.

"Of course they did," our teacher called out from

her office. "And no shouting in the corridor. Now off you go!"

Lexie burst out laughing as she punched the air and did a little leap. Carefully she pulled out her poster from her bag. "I'm going to ask Miss Dubois if I can copy this," she said, "then I can pin it up all over school!"

"You could ask her to mention it in registration, too," Nisha suggested.

"And get the other Year Seven form teachers to pass on the message," I added.

Lexie nodded vigorously. "I so hope enough girls sign up. I really want this to work!"

With that, Lexie set off in the direction of the staff room. She was on a mission. After break she raced into our history classroom just before Mr Wood and quickly sat down next to Nisha, out of breath. She had a small pile of posters with her.

Mr Wood called out for everyone to hand their homework books to the front for him to collect. Lexie flicked open her book, then slapped it shut and passed it forward, biting her lip. She turned to me and made a face.

"*D'accord*, everyone. Listen, please." Miss Dubois clapped her hands after she'd taken afternoon registration. "Lexie has an exciting announcement to make. Silence, *s'il vous plaît*."

Lexie stood at the front of the class next to Miss Dubois, gripping her poster.

Miss Dubois smiled at her and Lexie began. "I've decided to see if I can start a girls' Year Seven football team here at Priory Road," she began boldly. Lexie was never shy and she stood confidently looking out at the class. Some giggles rippled round the room as everyone read the poster Lexie was holding up. "Terrifying … I mean … Mrs Townsend has agreed to a taster session, so please, please sign your name in the space at the bottom of this poster if you want to give it a go. The fun's not just for boys, you know."

Jordan, who was captain of the Year Seven boys' team frowned. "Are you serious – a girls' team?" Lexie nodded defiantly and a couple of the boys jeered teasingly. "It sounds pretty embarrassing!"

"You'd all be too worried about getting muddy to play properly!" Tom piped up.

"Very funny, not," Lexie scowled.

"I certainly won't be signing up," Kirsty said,

wrinkling her button nose with distaste. "I can't think why anyone would!"

"Well, I want to!" Zophia piped up. "I think it's a brilliant idea, Lexie."

"I'll give it a go, too," Maisie added.

Lexie broke into a grin. "Don't forget to put your names down, then," she said, waving the poster as the bell went. There was a chorus of chairs scraping and feet trampling out of the room. A few of the girls gathered round Lexie. They quickly scribbled their names and walked away, chatting about the prospect of playing football. Lexie pinned up the poster on the form noticeboard and beamed at us. "This might just take off!"

Lexie's new mission really inspired me, so I got to our English classroom a bit early, hoping Mr Flight might be there already. I was in luck.

"Mr Flight?" I said. He looked over and smiled. I felt myself blush – what if he thought the idea was stupid? But it was too late to back out. "We've been doing a project for PSHE, about creating change."

"Oh yes?" Mr Flight said, his eyebrows raised.

"And, well, I'm doing my project on starting a school newspaper," I said in a bit of a rush, "and I was wondering whether I could actually do that? In real life, I mean. To give the students at Priory Road a voice…"

Mr Flight rubbed his chin, thinking for a moment. Then he nodded. "Giving the students of Priory Road a voice – written by students, for students. I like it."

I felt myself go even pinker.

"But a newspaper… It's a lot of work. It's quite complicated to coordinate, and it might be expensive to run, too." My face fell. Around me, the rest of the class began to come in. "There might be a way round that, though," he added quickly, seeing my crestfallen expression. "Why not start off with a blog? We could publish it on the school intranet. It's a very good idea. Well done, Ellie!"

I went to my seat, almost bursting with excitement.

"Nice one, Els," Jas smiled.

"Now I've actually got to write something! What if no one likes it? Pressure!" I whispered as Mr Flight started handing back our homework.

Jas gave me a look. "Ellie, your ideas are brilliant – trust me!"

At that moment Mr Flight handed me my

homework book back. I turned to the last page and smiled. "See?" Jas grinned. My creative writing had earned me an A. I was about to "yip" when I noticed the grim expression on Lexie's face – she sighed and closed her book, then slumped on the table.

"Does everyone understand what we're doing with this experiment?" Miss Dale, our chemistry teacher, asked, once we had all got settled and read the instructions on the board. We gave a general "Yes, Miss Dale".

"Good, now come and collect your equipment."

I rushed up with the rest of the class, then went back to the bench and got set up. We were working individually, goggles on, burning pasta, peanuts and marshmallows on the end of a long skewer over a Bunsen burner. We had test tubes firmly gripped by test-tube clamps and we had to measure the temperature of the water in the test tubes, after it had been heated by the food.

Miss Dale was busy at the back of the classroom, telling Zac off for eating the marshmallows that were meant for the experiment, when I heard Nisha squeak. I looked along the bench. Lexie's prong was overloaded with marshmallows, peanuts and pasta and the flame coming off them was getting bigger.

"You're not meant to burn all the food together, Lexie," Nisha whispered urgently.

"Really?" Lexie frowned. She looked away from the flame to read the instructions on the board, letting the skewer droop slightly.

"Watch out!" Maisie cried as it nearly touched the arm of her lab coat.

Lexie whipped up her skewer suddenly, and a burning marshmallow slipped off the end, landing on the bench, right on top of her book. The pages caught fire instantly. Kirsty, on the bench behind us, squealed loudly, then hurried to the end of her bench, as far away as possible. When the rest of the class saw the leaping flames, there was an outbreak of panic as everyone rushed to get away from it.

"Could everyone keep calm, please!" Miss Dale shouted above the squeals.

We huddled together, not wanting to venture near the flames and smoke rising from Lexie's book, as Miss Dale grabbed the fire extinguisher from the wall and pointed it at the book. The thick rush of water extinguished the flames with a damp fizzle, but it was not soon enough to stop the shrill blast of the fire alarm ringing.

Suddenly the whole school was spilling noisily out of classroom doors, pouring down the staircases and along corridors. We lined up in the playground in the drizzle, and waited to be checked off on the register.

"I'm going to be in so much trouble," Lexie groaned.

"It was an accident, though, Lex," Nisha said. "Miss Dale will understand that."

"You think?" Lexie asked, looking doubtful.

Nisha nodded unconvincingly.

"I bet she'll say I should've been paying more attention," Lexie added.

"Well, it could've been worse," I consoled her. "The bench might have caught fire, or even Maisie's hair! That would've been a disaster!"

"That's true," Lexie sighed. "I guess I'll just have to wait and see what Miss Dale says."

I glanced across our line, and caught sight of Ed. He looked up, and smiled. I couldn't stop myself returning it. I felt myself flush slightly and I quickly turned away, my heart rushing for a second.

My thoughts were interrupted by Jordan as he

called over from his place in the line.

"Nice one, Lexie," he grinned. "I'd have tried that myself if I'd thought of it!"

"I didn't do it on purpose!" Lexie tried to explain. But despite her explanations, Miss Dale gave her a lecture and a lunchtime detention.

School seemed pretty dull after the excitement with the fire, and even duller when Wiggy was teaching. He handed round our homework books at the end of class, just as we started packing away. I checked my mark and grimaced. Geography was not one of my favourite subjects, and even less so with Wiggy's unenthusiastic teaching style.

"Well, I'm glad my mum isn't going to see Wiggy at parents' evening," Jas sighed. "Not after that mark." She nodded towards Lexie's homework book. "How are your plans for The Adventure Forest coming along?"

"Not good," Lexie grumbled, shoving her book away. "It's just this PSHE project. It's taking up so much time to do it properly... I really am dreading parents' evening – at this rate it's going to be disastrous!"

"There's still time to pick it up," Nisha said, "and we're all here to help."

66

Play to Win

"Oh, it's not that I need help or anything," Lexie said quickly, looking a bit awkward, "I just need more time to fit everything in, that's all it is."

"Have you checked your football lists recently?" I asked, hoping that would take her mind off the doom and gloom of her schoolwork.

"Only every five seconds!" Nisha giggled.

"There are lots of names on the ones I've checked," she said, her usual enthusiasm returning in an instant. "I think everyone's had time to read them, so I better take them to Terrifying Townsend today! Actually, I'm going to collect the posters right now!"

With that, Lexie headed off at one hundred miles an hour down the corridor. She reappeared ten minutes later, holding a sheaf of posters.

"Seventeen names!" Lexie announced. "Do you think that's enough? Hang on a sec, though – what about you three?"

Me, Nisha and Jas looked at one another.

"Well, you know what a natural at sports I am, Lexie!" I said. "But … I suppose I'll have a go, if you two do as well."

"You're on," Jas grinned and Nisha nodded. "So that makes it twenty – twenty-one including you, Lexie!"

We went with Lexie to Terrifying Townsend's office and showed her the list.

"Looks like you've found something here, Lexie," she said with a satisfied nod. "Well done. I've checked my timetable already and I could fit in a taster session this Friday lunchtime. If that's successful we could set up a practice every Friday lunchtime and after school on Wednesday."

Terrifying Townsend sounded as enthusiastic as Lexie. As we walked away, Lexie couldn't keep the grin off her face.

7

Girls' football kicks off! And I come back down to earth with a bump...

"Where's Georgie?" Lexie asked, looking round. "Cat and Melissa aren't here, either."

We were standing on the football pitch, ready to begin the football taster session, shivering and feeling a bit self-conscious – some of the boys had come to see what was going on!

"Jade and Marcia aren't coming," said Aleisha, who was in a different form to us. She was swinging her arms about and jogging on the spot as she spoke. "They decided it was too cold!"

I was half wishing that I'd had the same idea, but before I had a chance to bottle it, Terrifying Townsend

69

strode over and blew her whistle. She took a quick head count. "Fifteen of you. Well, not bad."

Lexie looked disappointed at so many people dropping out, but kept quiet.

"It's Friday lunchtime, it's probably not the most popular," Jas whispered to her. Lexie nodded, but she kept glancing over in the direction of the changing rooms, even so, and Georgie did appear at the last minute, apologizing that her piano lesson had run over.

We started with warm-ups. We had to jog, run round cones and play "tag", but in a really organized way. Then we had a go at doing headers. I totally missed the ball when it was my turn, and it hit me on the shoulder. Jas ended up bashing her nose, causing a few laughs from a couple of the boys who still hadn't got bored of watching. Only Lexie and Aleisha headed it perfectly. Zophia was the surprise. She launched herself at the ball fearlessly and made a decent attempt at getting it back.

Next Terrifying Townsend gave us a short, sharp introduction to ball-control skills – how to dribble the ball round cones using the insides of our feet and trapping the ball under one foot. Then we looked at the basics of how to tackle, how to pass and how to shoot. Once we'd run through all of that, she split us into two groups and we had a mini match. Me and Nisha failed to even get near the ball. On the one occasion when it did fly towards me, I squealed and jumped out of the way, making everyone fall about giggling. Georgie and Aleisha were on our team, too, and Lexie and Jas were playing against us, along with Zophia.

Zophia and Georgie made up for their lack of experience with loads of enthusiasm. They were yelling for the ball and getting stuck in with their tackles. Lexie was streets ahead of most of the others, with one exception – Aleisha. Without Aleisha on our team, we would have been useless. She was lightning-quick, seriously competitive and she was a match for Lexie in skill.

Towards the end of the match, Lexie was close to scoring, but Aleisha intercepted the ball, and raced towards the other end. She took aim and hit a belter, right towards the goal. None of the defenders from the other team were in sight. Aleisha punched the air as the ball cruised past Jas, into the goal.

"Good timing, Aleisha! Excellent goal!" Terrifying Townsend yelled over. "Jas – pay attention!"

A moment later, the PE teacher blew her whistle and called everyone together.

"That was such good fun." Zophia beamed as we trooped back to the changing rooms. "I'm definitely signing up. Anyone else?" Zophia looked round eagerly.

I definitely wasn't, although I didn't want to break it to Lexie just yet. It was great to see her scheme coming together, but I couldn't wait to get out of my muddy, damp PE kit and back into my uniform.

"Aleisha looked like a natural on the pitch, didn't she?" Nisha said as we took our seats in PSHE that afternoon.

Lexie shrugged.

"What's up?" Jas asked. "I thought you'd be happy to have great players!"

"I am," Lexie said quickly. "But, oh, I don't know. I just hoped that I'd be top of something, for once. Especially as it was all my idea!"

"But if Aleisha's good," Nisha pointed out, "it'll help make a really strong team."

"I know," Lexie said with a sigh. "Come on, we

better get out our projects."

After putting an abrupt end to the subject, Lexie was quiet for the rest of the lesson. She worked on putting together her storyboard. Mr Blaxhall had said she could submit an actual video for the advert if she wanted to, so she was laying out the sequence in minute detail. I decided to write one of my first articles.

I sat for a second, chewing my pen as I wondered which article to write first. Then I grinned, and began to scribble:

Football fever strikes Priory Road! There was a talent overload on the pitch at lunchtime today, when the Year Seven girls turned up for their first ever girls-only football taster session.

The words flowed and I wrote the last sentence, just as Mr Blaxhall asked us to finish.

"Do you three fancy coming over to mine tomorrow for a bit?" Lexie asked as we packed up at the end of the class.

"Oooh, what for?" Jas asked.

"Nothing much," Lexie said, trying to sound off-hand. "Maybe we could get in a bit of extra training before the next football practice, that's all. Terrifying Townsend said it was going to be Wednesday after school."

My heart fell. "I don't know, Lexie," I said. "I've got swimming practice tonight and after this lunchtime, all I want to do is drop! And I've got to get this mock newspaper finished, too."

"We don't have to be out for ages," Lexie pleaded. "Just a bit, just to..."

"To what?" Nisha asked.

"To help me get the edge over Aleisha?" Lexie ventured guiltily, waiting for our reactions. Jas and Nisha groaned. "Please? I'd do the same for you... And Demba Keshi said practice is key, and I really want to get somewhere with this."

"If it's important to you, of course we'll come," Jas said. "But don't get hung up about Aleisha – it's great that you're both good."

"I know," Lexie said as lightly as she could manage. "But it'll help the team if I get better, too, won't it?"

Nisha looked at me and Jas, and then at Lexie. "Actually, Lexie, I need to talk to you about something..."

Lexie looked panicked, but she didn't say anything, and waited to hear what Nisha was going to tell her.

Play to Win

Nisha continued. "Well, you know I started photography club? It's on a Wednesday after school ... so I won't be able to make the football sessions. Otherwise, I'd totally be there... But I love photography, and I'm only just getting started!"

Lexie looked deflated – she had been filled with enthusiasm and energy for the football team just moments before.

"Anyway," Nisha said cheerfully, "you saw me play at the taster session – I was useless! The team will be much better off without me!"

Lexie smiled at this and laughed. "Well, there was definitely room for improvement... Will you still come at the weekend, though, Nish? It won't be so much fun without you!"

"Nisha!" Lexie called out. "You've already taken about a hundred photos of squirrels, do you need another one?"

"It's for my nature-trail project," Nisha called back, "I told you! And for the photography competition!"

"You said you've already got loads of photos," Lexie said crossly. "And anyway, can't you think about that later?"

Lexie was jogging backwards. Me and Jas were just behind her. Jas's bouncy, ringletted hair had flopped and my cheeks were bright red. I stopped for a second and stroked Jinx, who trotted up to me. We'd met up at Lexie's house, but she'd ushered us straight out for a jog with Smarty and Jinx to improve our fitness. Only Lexie, who was in the cross-country club at school, had a slightly different idea about fitness to the rest of us. Nisha took one more photo, then ran over to us. We jogged on for a few more minutes in pained silence until Jas collapsed on the bench near the park café. I joined her in an instant.

"At this rate I'm going to be too exhausted for the performing arts class tomorrow!" Jas said. "I really want to make a good impression, as it's the first day!"

Lexie spotted that we'd given up and jogged over to us. "Guys, come on!" Lexie said. She was hardly even out of breath. "You're not taking this seriously!"

Finally Jas snapped. "Look, Lexie, we're happy to support you and everything," she said, "but football and being better than Aleisha is your passion – not ours."

Lexie looked from Jas to me.

"Jas is right," I added. "Sorry, Lexie. I mean, I'm happy to try something new, but getting yelled at by

Play to Win

Terrifying Townsend isn't my idea of a fun Friday lunchtime..."

Lexie looked over to where Luke and his mates were playing a game. "Well, I guess you're right," she finally said. "Sorry, guys, that's a bit like expecting me to join reading club or something."

"So, does that mean the torture's over now?" Jas grinned. "Can we go back?"

Lexie nodded and gave one final glance over to the boys.

"Why don't you ask if you could join in?" I asked.

But Lexie shook her head. "Luke wouldn't want me hanging around with him, not in front of his friends," she sighed. "Come on, let's go. Can we at least jog back? With no photographic pauses?"

She called the dogs over and we all set off together at a steady pace. Just before we got to the gate of the park, Smarty darted straight in front of my path, his attention caught by something in the bushes. I tried to dodge round him at the last second and stepped on a patch of uneven ground. My ankle twisted and I stumbled, landing with a thud. I grasped my ankle with both hands as my BFFs rushed to my side.

"Where's the wounded soldier?" Dad asked when he got to Lexie's about half an hour later.

I'd been trying to pretend it didn't hurt, but when I saw him I was so relieved that I suddenly burst into tears! I hopped to the car, with Jas's help. Mrs Jones had put a bag of frozen peas on my ankle, but it was still swollen and it really ached, so Dad took me to the walk-in clinic to get it checked out. When we eventually got in to see the doctor it was good news – it was just a sprain, so I had to rest it and be careful not to put my full weight on it.

We had dinner in front of the television for once – I was never normally allowed! My phone kept lighting up with text after text from my worried BFFs. I couldn't do much, so I thought it would be the ideal time to have a go at writing my first blog post.

Hi, and welcome to my very first blog! My name's Ellie and I'm a Year Seven. When I first started at Priory Road that was a kind of embarrassing thing to admit - no one wants to be the newbie. But I'm pretty small, so it was hard to pretend I

Play to Win

was anything else. Anyway, this year's turned out to be pretty cool after all, and now I want to celebrate all things Year Seven. So, this blog is going to be dedicated to finding out and sharing how some of us Year Sevens spend our time both inside and outside of the humungous school gates. Hope you enjoy it!

I went to bed early, with a book, but my mind kept pinging with ideas for the blog. So in the end I gave up trying to read, got the notebook from my bedside table and scribbled down lots of notes. I couldn't wait to wake up in the morning and get them written up! Suddenly my phone went. It was Jas, again!

Can't sleep! 1st class tomoz – yippee! Wish me luck! Want it 2 b morning NOW!!!

I leaned back against the pillow and quickly texted back.

You don't need luck – you'll rock! Break a leg! xx

Jas's performing arts class would be a perfect blog

subject! I made a note of it, then turned off the light. The idea of lots of Priory Roaders reading my blog made me really excited, not scared or nervous in the slightest.

The next morning my ankle was all stiff and I didn't really fancy getting out of bed. Dad brought me up some breakfast and after that I stayed curled up with my notebook, writing ideas for the blog. I dozed off to sleep again, and was woken by the sound of the doorbell. I checked my watch – it was nearly three o'clock! I could hear muffled voices and footsteps creeping up the stairs. Suddenly the door swung open and in burst Jas, Lexie and Nisha.

"We've come to check on the invalid!" Nisha said.

"And we come bearing gifts," Jas added theatrically.

Lexie put a basket down on the floor and pulled a blanket out of it. Then she produced a couple of flasks, some plastic cups and plates. Jas and Nisha grabbed Tupperware boxes filled with sandwiches, sausage rolls and veggie samosas. Another one was filled with muffins, freshly baked by Nisha.

"We thought you might need cheering up," Lexie said as she spread out the blanket on my bedroom floor. I manoeuvred myself out of bed and on to the floor with the others. Lexie passed me a card. It was handmade, with a picture of all four of us on the front.

"Thanks, guys – this is just what I needed!"

"So, have you made your decision then about the football team?" Lexie grinned.

"Er, yes," I laughed. "I'll definitely stick to blogging about it in future, rather than trying to play!"

8

A blog is born and Lexie has some serious explaining to do...

"I can't believe you get to sit PE out!" Jas groaned, looking at me enviously as I hobbled off to sit in the office for the lesson. It almost made falling over worth it! As they played netball, I sat and worked on my next blog post. Jas had filled me in on her performing arts class, and I couldn't wait to write about it. I slid my notebook out, and put my pen to the blank page.

It isn't just the girls' football team, or this blog, that has come about because of Inspiration Week. Self-professed Drama Queen, Jasmine Cole, was so inspired by Saffy Fine's appearance at drama club

82

Play to Win

that barely a week later she was enrolled at a performing arts class! Her ambition? To make it as a children's television presenter one day, just like Saffy.

But first comes the training! Jas joined the Sunday class at the Shining Star Academy in town. Her first session was jam-packed; she got to try choreographed dance, physical comedy and singing. She even got to try some screen acting, too! Apparently everyone was really welcoming and it's made her even more determined to fulfil her dreams - first step Shining Star Academy, next step world domination in kids' TV!

And where did Jas's dreams of being a star start? Well, it might have had something to do with a certain talent show that she started in her very first term at Priory Road!

I carried on writing, smiling as I thought about the talent show. Only Jas could come up with an idea that crazy. She'd pulled it off, too. Well, with a huge helping hand from Miss Dubois. That made me think about all the Year Sevens getting involved in the school production of *Oliver!*, too. There was so much to write about! I showed Mr Flight my long list of possible topics to cover in English, later that day.

"Excellent, Ellie, sniffing out a story like a true journalist!" Mr Flight snapped his fingers, looking excited. "If you hand in these first blog entries to me today, I'll put up a notice in the foyer and ask the form teachers to spread the word across the school. And we can monitor the traffic and see how popular it is! But for this blog to really capture the imagination of the other students, you're going to need to cover topics that have appeal across the board."

"Er, in what way?" I asked, unsure what he meant.

"I mean that we'll need to include the boys' perspective, too," Mr Flight smiled. "After all, this is a mixed school. I'll leave that with you to ponder."

"I'm on it," I said, going pink at the prospect of having to interview some of the boys.

"We can get some of the older students to write blogs for their years, too. Ellie, this is a really good project for the school – well done again."

As I sat back down, I whispered to Jas. "Did you hear that?"

"What?" Jas replied.

Play to Win

"Mr Flight wants me to involve some of the boys in the blog!" I cringed.

"No way!" Jas said, grinning. "Wait a minute... I know! What about Ed and his skateboarding? He's always going on about it. I bet he'd be good."

"And Ajay and Travis's band," I added quickly, trying to stop myself going totally fuchsia at the mention of Ed. "Will you come with me? When I interview any of the boys, I mean."

"Course!" Jas grinned. "It'll be fun!"

I wasn't going to go along to Lexie's advert shoot after school because I was still hobbling about on my swollen ankle, but my BFFs wouldn't hear of it.

"We need your artistic input," Nisha said.

It was the talk of a hot chocolate that finally decided me. "OK, but I might just have to give you my input from the bench," I said, smiling.

We were on our way out when Jas nudged me. "Oooh, look!"

Me, Lexie and Nisha glanced over to where Jas was pointing. There was a new, colourful A4 poster on the noticeboard. On it was written:

My BFFs all patted me on the back as I stood there biting my lip while I read it. Then I couldn't stop grinning.

"My name's on a poster!" I squeaked, feeling slightly hot.

The next second Ed and Zac walked past.

"You're famous, Woody!" Ed whooped. On the very first day at Priory Road, Ed had decided to give me a nickname. It started off as 'Woodworm' (my surname is Lovewood), and had since morphed into Woody. It wasn't that bad, really. In fact, I secretly quite liked it.

Play to Win

Lexie had chosen a Monday evening for filming her advert because she knew that the park would be pretty much empty, and we'd be able to get it done without having Jordan or his friends interfering. She had written out everything that Jas had to say. The aim of the advert was to show that girls could be good at football, too, but also that it wasn't so much fun on your own. There was one very special guest star – Jas's brother Josh.

"So, what's this for again?" he asked, grinning at the camera. "Am I going to be famous...?"

"I told you," Jas sighed. "It's for this PSHE project we're doing."

"Come on, then. I've got places to be."

"What, like home?" Jas teased.

"So what if it is, sis?" Josh smiled. "Our dinner will be waiting! And just remember, you all owe me for this."

He started playing football with Lexie, letting her use him to show the way she could tackle and control the ball, or how she could take the ball off him. When she'd finished and Jas had stopped her commentary, he grinned. "You're actually not bad."

"What, for a girl?" Lexie asked, going off script for

a moment as she stood with her foot on the ball. Nisha kept her camera pointing at the pair.

"Girl, boy, it doesn't matter – you're pretty good," he added with a shrug. Then, just as Lexie puffed herself up for a second, Josh seized the moment and tapped the ball from under her foot and dribbled it away, laughing. Lexie gave chase, but she couldn't catch him up. Josh brought the ball back at speed, stopping with a skid in front of the camera. "I've still got two years on her, though."

Nisha stopped the filming. "That's a wrap!"

"Thanks, Josh, that was awesome," Lexie said.

"*I* was awesome, you mean," Josh joked. "Right, I'm off, you two coming?"

"Yes, sure!" I said, smiling. When we had first started at Priory Road, Josh didn't want anything to do with us. Now he was actually offering to get the bus with us – that was serious progress!

Jas nodded. "We better get going. See you both tomorrow!"

We left Lexie and Nisha looking at the footage on the camera as we waved goodbye. Jas linked arms with me and helped me to keep the weight off my bad ankle as we headed out of the park to the bus stop.

Play to Win

☆ ✭ ☆

Nisha got out her camera after our last lesson the next day. We sat for a moment, and watched the video. It was fab, and the bit at the end with Josh worked brilliantly.

"It's perfect!" Lexie hugged Nisha.

"You're pretty good in front of the camera, Lexie," I said. "Mrs Crawfield would be proud! Why don't we show her in drama club?"

Lexie's face dropped. "Actually, I've decided that I can't carry on with drama club. Well, I say I, but what I mean is that Mum and Dad don't think I should."

"How come?" I asked.

"They reminded me about my promise to improve my marks," Lexie said, in a bored voice. "Now I've got football practice on a Wednesday as well as netball matches and cross-country running, I haven't got any time left for homework. Mum and Dad said something had to give. The worst thing is that it's parents' evening next week and I'm really worried that they're expecting some kind of miracle with my work. But it's not going to happen. I think I can kiss goodbye to The Adventure Forest."

"That's rubbish," Jas sighed. She'd been looking forward to it almost as much as Lexie.

"Well, looks like it'll just be the three of us for drama club, then," I sighed, feeling a bit disappointed.

"Oh, um, make that two," Nisha said, looking sheepish. "My mum and Dave said pretty much the same as Lexie's parents – now I've got photography club on Wednesdays after school they said I had to choose which one I wanted to do most. I like drama, but I love photography. Sorry, guys."

"Just me and you, then," Jas said, looking at me.

"And Ed," Lexie giggled, grabbing her coat. "Don't forget Ed."

I decided to take the opportunity at drama club to ask Ed if I could interview him about skateboarding. I dragged Jas with me to go and talk to him as we were all leaving.

Jas started the conversation. "I can't believe you didn't audition for our play last term, your piece was really good today."

I expected some kind of wise-guy reply, but Ed just shrugged and said, "I didn't think I'd be any good."

He didn't say anything else and I stood there awkwardly. This was the perfect moment to ask him about doing an interview for the blog! I blushed scarlet and Jas nudged me. Finally, I managed to get some words out. "I was wondering about doing a piece on skateboarding for my blog…"

"Yeah, that'd be cool. Why don't you come down to the skate park? I'm going this Sunday afternoon, so you could meet me there? About three?" Ed said, suddenly going a bit pink himself. He grabbed his coat and headed out. "See you then!"

Even though I was safely out of the football team, I said I'd go and watch the Friday lunchtime practice to get some material for my blog entry. The girls were warming up and I stood shivering by the edge of the pitch, wrapped up in my fluffy hooded coat. It was raining lightly, so I tucked my notebook into my pocket.

I looked over to the school, wondering if I could get away with watching through a classroom window, but I knew it wouldn't be the same.

Terrifying Townsend's foghorn voice called the girls together. "We're going to play a five-a-side match, and I want you to impress me," she barked. "From what I see today, I'm going to pick the team to play our first competitive game. It's going to be against Freethorpe next Wednesday after school. I'll pin up a list of the final team, plus reserves, outside the changing rooms at the end of the day. Now, let's divide you into teams. Lexie, I want you to captain the red side. Aleisha, you'll captain the blues."

I noticed Lexie glance over to Aleisha, eyeing her up like she was some kind of arch-rival. The rest of the girls stood waiting as Terrifying Townsend picked out two teams. She organized the girls into their positions, then blew her whistle fiercely. For the next fifteen minutes the pitch was a blur of girls running up and down, breathless, muddied and determined.

"Come on, reds!" Lexie shouted crossly as Maisie missed a back pass and Aleisha took possession. Aleisha glanced up the pitch, then booted the ball up to the far end, where Georgie was waiting near goal. She quietly got the ball under control, turned and blasted it with her right foot between the posts. Sammy, the goalie, dived the wrong way. The blues cheered and high-fived while Lexie scowled. She grabbed the ball, urging on her team as she raced back to the centre circle to kick off and get the game going again. Fired up, her pony tail bobbing furiously, she set off up the pitch, passing to Zophia, who rushed past Tabitha. Zophia was going for goal, but at the last second she tried to dodge round Aleisha and tripped on the ball.

Lexie shouted out for the team to concentrate. Then as Aleisha ran with the ball, tapping it along, Lexie went in for a tackle. For a second both girls scrapped on the ball. Aleisha was strong and feisty, and not about to give up. The two of them tugged each other's shirts before Lexie finally pulled away, only to get a blast of the whistle.

"Foul!"

Lexie was about to argue, but the look on Terrifying Townsend's face told her not to even think about it. Instead, Lexie redoubled her efforts. She flitted all over the pitch, tackling and making some spectacular passes and shots on goal. But she was equalled by Aleisha at every move. When Zophia finally converted a pass to score, the reds were still behind, 2–1. Terrifying Townsend checked her watch, then blasted the whistle.

"Well done, everyone," Terrifying Townsend said, sounding unusually pleased. "The team will be posted after the final bell."

Lexie was pink, her dark pony tail slicked to her face with a combination of rain and sweat. I hobbled back in with everyone, but I could tell that Lexie was in a bad mood.

"So, who do you reckon's going to be picked as captain for next week?" Tabitha asked as we reached the changing rooms.

"I really hope I've got a chance," Aleisha beamed.

Lexie looked up. "But this whole thing was my idea," she said, suddenly changing the atmosphere in the changing room. "I think Mrs Townsend will pick me..."

Aleisha raised her eyebrows, her smile fading. "It should be made on ability, not whose idea it was."

"That's OK then," Lexie snapped, "because it would still be me."

Aleisha's face dropped in disbelief. "This is meant to be a team game, Lexie, in case you forgot. And I thought it was going to be fun. But if you're going to be a diva about it, you can shove your football team. I'm out of it!"

Aleisha stormed out of the changing rooms and the door swung shut with a bang. Lexie looked at me, a bit red-faced. "I hardly think I'm the diva round here, do you?"

"Um, you might have gone a bit far..." I said tentatively. "You're both really good."

That clearly wasn't what Lexie wanted me to say. She sighed crossly and turned away.

Lexie stayed pretty quiet after that, but as the afternoon dragged on, her grump soon turned to worry. She fidgeted all through French and rushed off to check the board the moment the bell rang. We followed after her. There was no sign of Aleisha. Terrifying Townsend appeared from her office and pinned up the team list. Lexie's name was second on the list and Aleisha's was at the top – she'd been picked as captain. Lexie's shoulders slumped. Then she turned to face Terrifying Townsend, with a look of slight dread on her face.

"Oh, um, Mrs Townsend," Lexie said. "Aleisha quit the team."

Terrifying Townsend looked surprised. "What do you mean, she's quit?"

I noticed Lexie gulp. I think I would have run away from those glaring eyes, but Lexie was braver.

"Er, we had a bit of a falling-out," Lexie admitted, looking away.

"About?" Terrifying Townsend asked.

"About who should be captain," Lexie said quietly.

"You need to shape up," Terrifying Townsend growled as she crossed through Aleisha's name on the list. "You wanted this, Lexie. Don't let petty differences ruin it."

Lexie stood miserably, as Mrs Townsend walked away. She had got her wish of being captain, but she knew it was bad news for the team.

"Why did you argue about it in the first place?" Nisha asked, looking at Lexie like she was crazy. "It's not like you."

"I know," Lexie sighed. "I just really wanted to be captain, I guess, that's all."

Lexie's eyes glistened. The look on her face said it all. She knew she'd messed up big time, and no words from her BFFs were going to change that.

Lexie blurts out a challenge she might just regret...

When Sunday arrived, I felt a flutter of butterflies in my stomach. It wouldn't be long before I was heading off to the skate park to meet Ed. I was so grateful that Jas was coming with me. She had her performing arts course in the morning, and I was going to meet up with her in town afterwards. Nisha was going to come along for a bit, too, to take some photos.

I'd spent ages preparing questions to ask Ed. I wanted him to think they were interesting and exciting. That way, he might think I was the same… I looked in the mirror, and couldn't stop a small smile. Since when had I wanted to impress Ed? I practised asking my questions, still looking at the mirror, repeating them a few times in different ways.

"Ugh, that question's lame," I said quietly to myself, hastily scribbling one out. Then I added in another few.

I'd just put my pen down, feeling my heart flutter with nervous excitement, when Mum called up the stairs. "Ellie! Would you like a lift into town? Me and Dad are going to pop in to buy some food for dinner tonight."

"Yes, please!" I called back down. I opened my wardrobe and flipped through my clothes. I had put on a dress and leggings this morning, but at the last minute I changed my mind. I didn't want anyone at the skate park to think I looked too dressed up! In the end I opted for purple jeans, black boots and a thick woollen black jumper with a snowflake pattern on the front. I changed quickly, checked how I looked in the mirror and then hurried downstairs.

"Got your mobile?" Dad asked. I nodded. "Ring me from the park when you've finished and I'll come and pick you and Jas up."

"Thanks, Dad," I said. My heart was hammering. I was about to conduct my first interview! With Ed! Nerves were tingling all through me on the drive into town, but as soon as I caught sight of Jas waiting outside the shopping centre entrance, I felt better.

"Have fun," Mum called as I hopped out of the car.

Jas broke into a huge grin when she saw me, then suddenly started pretending to be a robot.

"Jas, you're freaking me out!" I giggled. "What're you doing? How did this morning go?"

"We're learning about physical comedy," Jas said. Her face lit up with happiness. "I loved it so much, it's just the best thing ever!"

We had a hot chocolate in the Ace Diner so Jas could tell me all about the class. She even showed me some of the moves that she'd learned. "Miss Deveraux, the group leader, is incredible! She used to be a trapeze artist in *Cirque du Soleil*!"

After we'd finished, we walked the short distance towards the skate park.

"Look! There's Ed!" Jas grinned, nudging me. He was on the ramp. He had on a pair of baggy combat trousers, and a hoody. He waved as he saw us and jumped off his board, flipping one end up and catching it.

"He actually looks pretty cool," Jas said, sounding surprised.

"Kind of," I agreed, going pink. Jas nudged me, but thankfully she kept quiet, for once!

"Ready to write the best blog post ever?" Ed asked, smiling. I smiled back, trying to cover up my nerves as I got out my notebook and found the page with my questions on.

I looked round. "Should we go and sit on the edge of the ramp over there to do the interview?"

Ed nodded. Jas came with us, but kept herself out of the way, trying to run up the ramp.

"Right. So, Ed, how did you get into skateboarding?"

As the conversation got going, my nerves disappeared. We chatted about how Ed got started, what tricks he could do (and which one he wanted to learn most). He told me why he loved it, how difficult it was and who taught him. I scribbled like mad. Ed became really passionate when he told me about the money needed to restore the park.

"It used to be a real hub for everyone – not just skaters," he explained as Jas came and sat next to us. "Rollerbladers, BMXers – everyone used to hang out and there was a really friendly vibe about the place. But it's just falling apart. The council's trying to do something about it – I read that the other day when I was researching my project – but they say there's no funding, so that's it. The end."

Ed looked round, his skateboard balanced over his knees. "Come on, I'll show you both some moves."

At that moment, Nisha ran up and, after a quick hello, she started snapping away. Ed tried to show us how to do an ollie, but we could barely keep our balance. My ankle was still a bit stiff, but I just ignored it – I didn't want to miss out on my first go at skateboarding!

"This is so much harder than it looks!" I giggled, almost wobbling off. It made Ed's confidence on the board seem even more impressive. As he showed us some more moves, Nisha captured some brilliant action shots.

"They'll look perfect on the blog!" I smiled as I shaded the pale sun from my eyes and looked at the screen.

"I might even be able to use them for the competition!" Nisha beamed.

"When do you think you'll write the blog post, Ellie?" Ed asked. "I can't wait to read it – it's bound to be good."

"Because Ellie wrote it?" Jas asked, smiling at me.

"Because it's all about me!" Ed laughed.

Ed's phone beeped and he checked the message, then dropped his skateboard to the floor.

"Gotta go," he explained. "My mates are waiting. Laters."

"Thanks, Ed," I called out as he jumped on his board and rode off.

At the entrance to the park, we saw him meet his mum and little sister. We looked at each other and giggled – they weren't quite the mates that we'd had in mind.

"He was trying to impress you, Ellie!" Nisha said.

"You know, without Zac encouraging him to be a baboon," Jas smiled, "Ed's quite sweet."

"He really is," I agreed.

Nisha and Jas both turned to look at me, grinning. I couldn't help breaking out into a smile, too.

That evening I started to write up the interview, leafing through my notes.

Today I got to hang out with a skateboarding star! Well, a Year Seven skateboarding star, anyway. I even got to have a go on the board, too. But did I manage to master an ollie? You'll have to read on to find out!

Play to Win

I felt a warm glow as I began to write about Ed. Crumble jumped up on to my desk, and shuffled his head under my arm. I scooped him up and gave him a cuddle. "Oh, Crumble," I laughed. "What is going on?"

As the girls' first match drew nearer, Lexie actually began to feel some nerves mixed in among the excitement. When Wednesday arrived, she couldn't think about anything else.

"Why wasn't I happy just letting Aleisha be captain?" Lexie groaned at the end of the day as we headed for the changing rooms.

"You'll be fine," Nisha reassured her. "Just enjoy it."

"Lexie's normally so calm and collected about sports competitions," Jas frowned. "How come she's freaked by this one? She loves football!"

"That's probably why – maybe she wants to win too much?" I suggested as me and Jas pulled on our coats.

"I guess that's possible," Nisha agreed. "Anyway, I better get to photography club. Enjoy the match!"

Me and Jas linked arms and headed outside on to the playing fields to watch.

The girls from Freethorpe trooped out on to the

playing fields. Minutes later, Terrifying Townsend led Lexie and our team from the changing room. A small group of us waited by the edge of the pitch. Kirsty and Eliza had appeared briefly, but after waiting for a few moments in the cold and noticing that there were no boys watching, they gave up and left. Jo-Jo and Ali, the reserves, were standing near us in their kit. Molly and Trin were there to support Zophia and Tabitha. Nemone and Saskia were there out of curiosity. Over on the other side of the playing fields, the Year Seven boys' football practice was going on.

While we waited for the game to start, Saskia leaned forward and grinned at me. "I've been reading your blog, Ellie. It's really good fun. I'm amazed no one's thought of doing this before now!"

"I've been reading it, too!" Trin joined in. "It made me laugh, thinking back over some of the stuff that's happened this year. I can't wait for the next post!"

"Wow!" I said, breaking into a wide smile. "I was wondering if anyone had read it or not. Thanks!"

"My sister said she's planning to write a Year Nine blog post," Nemone added. "She was talking about it with all of her friends, too."

I was really excited that the blog was starting to take

Play to Win

off! Jas grinned at me, and we turned our attention back to the pitch.

Terrifying Townsend flipped a coin to see who'd start with the ball, and Freethorpe won the toss. Then she blew the whistle. The match was underway! The Freethorpe team played as a tight group, and it wasn't long before they scored.

Lexie clapped her hands to galvanize her team. "Come on, Priory – keep trying!"

But by half-time they were trailing 4–0. The second half wasn't much better. Lexie tried to reach every cross and threw herself into every tackle. But she got frustrated when she hit passes and the other players weren't looking or ran the wrong way. As yet another goal skidded past Sammy into Priory Road's net, I noticed Aleisha at the school fence, watching intently. She was almost out of view. The next second Georgie managed to claw one goal back in a muddled tangle of legs. When I looked over at the fence again, Aleisha had disappeared. In the remaining minutes, Freethorpe increased their lead. When the final whistle blew, the score was a dismal 9–1.

"It was only a friendly, remember," Maisie said, puffing as she came off the pitch, covered in mud, "and it was our first ever match. We're bound to get better." But her attempt to console Lexie wasn't getting far.

"We were totally outplayed," Lexie sighed.

I heard laughter and turned to see that the boys' team had finished their practice. As our team left the pitch, heads down, the boys wandered over. They clearly couldn't wait to stick the boot in.

"Maybe you should stick to netball," Jordan said smugly.

Lexie glowered at him. Her face was pink and streaked with mud. Once the boys had walked off, she turned to us. "It looks like my attempts to get a girls' football team at Priory Road might be doomed already," she groaned.

"Well, at least you tried," Jas said. "And you're ace at cross-country and netball – isn't that enough?"

Lexie turned on Jas. "No way!" she burst out. "I don't love them like I love football. You three all have things that you love and they're going amazingly – your blog's really popular, Ellie; Jas, you're doing your performing arts class and Nisha's loving her photography. Football means the world to me and the whole thing is about to fail!"

Play to Win

Tears of frustration welled up in her eyes. As I put my arm round Lexie's shoulders, Luke walked up. He was about to speak to Lexie, when Jordan walked past again with a couple of other boys.

"See, this is why girls shouldn't play football," he smirked to the others. "They cry when they lose. Boo-hoo!"

Luke stood awkwardly next to Lexie, looking caught between her and Jordan.

Lexie scowled and roughly wiped the tears from her face. A look of steely determination came into her blue eyes.

"Girls can be just as good as boys at football," she said, "and I'll ... I'll prove it to you!"

"You reckon?" Jordan laughed.

"How'll you do that, then?" Tom asked.

"I challenge you to a match – girls v boys!" Lexie burst out. "And we'll win!"

"You're on!" Jordan smiled.

What on earth had Lexie just let herself in for?

Year Seven parents' evening – cringe!

It was Thursday morning, and the spectre of parents' evening loomed large. But right now, Lexie had marginally more scary things on her mind. Jordan was looking over, and whispering to a few of the other boys in registration. Zac let out a guffaw.

"So, do you think I was a bit rash?" Lexie asked.

"Maybe just a little," Jas suggested. Lexie groaned and sank into her chair.

At that moment, Ajay and Travis came in to the classroom.

"Ooh, wish me luck!" I said to my BFFs, then I got up and went over to the boys. "Hi! Could I interview you about your band, for my blog?" I asked. I had handed my skateboarding blog over to Mr Flight already and I couldn't wait to get on with my next entry – I just hoped that the band liked the idea, too!

"Sure! Do you want to watch us rehearsing this weekend?" Ajay offered. "Then you can actually see us and hear us in action. We meet up every Saturday at one o'clock."

"That would be amazing, thanks, Ajay!" I beamed. I felt a rush of excitement – I couldn't quite believe how much I was getting out and about for the blog! Word had spread, and people were actually coming up to me and saying how cool it was, and how they'd enjoyed reading it. People were even suggesting ideas for new topics. Saskia and Nemone had said I could go and watch them train for the cheerleading team, and Lauren asked if I wanted to spend a day at the local riding stables with her. At this rate they were going to have to wait till after the Easter holidays!

At break, Lexie decided she couldn't put it off any longer, and went to visit Terrifying Townsend's office. While Lexie went in, we loitered just behind her.

"Year Seven girls versus boys?" she said, sounding doubtful. Nisha stepped forward. "It could be a charity match, with all the profits going to a local cause?"

"I know!" I suddenly jumped in. "It could be in aid of the local skate park!"

Terrifying Townsend looked grim. She always did when she was thinking. But then her face slowly lightened. "I'll talk to Mr Lawrence about it."

Mr Lawrence was head of PE. Lexie gulped.

"These things take a fair bit of organizing to make them a success," Terrifying Townsend continued, "so we would need to work out how to interest a large audience. That way we'll have lots of spectators, and raise a good amount of money..." She paused, then she actually smiled. "I know! He might like the idea of a second match – the senior school team versus the teachers. Now that would be fun!"

We looked at each other and smiled, half unable to believe what we were hearing. Maybe Mrs Townsend wasn't so terrifying after all!

It was weird seeing everyone in the foyer that evening with their parents for the parents' evening. The whole of Year Seven looked embarrassed. I was standing in the foyer with my BFFs and our parents, waiting for the appointments to start. Lexie looked pale and fidgety, like she couldn't wait to get the next hour over with, but at the same time, she never wanted it to start!

"Shall we try and meet back here afterwards?" Nisha asked. We nodded. "Wish me luck," Nisha grinned, before heading off with her mum and step-dad.

"I don't know how long I'll be here," Jas said. "Josh is babysitting Lulu, and Mum doesn't want to be too long."

Unable to delay it any longer, I set off with Mum and Dad. Our first appointment was with Mr Flight. He gave the most positive report about my work, but all the other subject teachers said I was doing OK, too. Mr Wood was complimentary about my history work and Miss Dubois said how encouraging it was to see me growing in confidence!

"I'm really impressed, Ellie; all your teachers said you always tried your hardest," Dad said, smiling and ruffling my hair.

"Dad!" I squirmed. "Not here!" But I was happy that they were pleased.

Nisha was back in the foyer already. She'd had good reports, too.

Jas had texted:

Gone home – got a gd report mostly (maths – yuk!) c u tomoz, hope all ok! what about The Adventure Forest??!!

Then Lexie, Luke and their parents reappeared in the foyer. Lexie said something to her parents, then came over to us.

"So, spill! How did it go?" Nisha asked. By the look on her face, we could already guess the answer.

"Totally terrible," Lexie sighed. "My cause wasn't exactly helped by Luke getting glowing reports all round. It didn't start too badly, because we saw Mrs Townsend first. She said that I'd showed determination, and that I had potential to go far."

"Well, that sounds ace!" I said.

"Maybe, but it went downhill pretty quickly after that," Lexie said sheepishly. "And, um," Lexie paused for a moment, like the words had got stuck in her throat. "Um, Miss Dubois asked if I struggled to understand what was being asked in lessons."

Lexie glanced up at us. She looked worried that we were going to laugh at her. She should have known us

112

better than that.

"So, what did you say?" Nisha asked.

Lexie made a face. "I kept quiet at first, but Mum and Dad wouldn't let it go. I admitted in the end that I'm finding the work hard sometimes. I mean, it just takes me a bit longer to get stuff, and by that time the lesson's moved on and then I'm confused. I hate it when I don't get something and everyone else does. I thought it might get easier this term. Only it hasn't."

"Why didn't you tell us?" Nisha asked.

Lexie shrugged. "It's not exactly the kind of thing you want to advertise."

I felt terrible that Lexie had been keeping that a secret for so long.

"Miss Dubois was really nice, though," Lexie continued. "She said that I shouldn't be worried about taking longer to 'process information' – not everyone does it at the same speed. She's going to tell the teachers to give me more time and help."

"Oh, Lexie, we'll do everything we can to help you, too," I said.

Lexie sighed again and looked over to her parents. "Compared to Luke's, my report was pretty terrible, so

I'm not holding my breath that The Adventure Forest is going to happen. Sorry, guys…"

Lexie's parents were in deep discussion with Mr Wood and Miss Dubois. By the look on their faces, I thought that Lexie might be right.

Nisha put her arm round Lexie. "Well, you don't know that yet, so let's wait and see. And anyway, we'll definitely find something fun to do for your birthday, even if it's not that."

Lexie eats a portion of humble pie ... and the football team get a PLAN!

First thing on Friday, Lexie bounded into the cloakroom. "You'll never guess what!" she said, wrenching off her coat and hanging it up. She didn't even give us a chance to guess, she was so eager to tell us. "Mum and Dad have said yes to The Adventure Forest!" Lexie did a little jig. "They hadn't realized that I was finding my schoolwork difficult. In fact, they feel pretty bad that they didn't pick up on anything sooner! And guess what?"

"Don't keep asking!" Jas giggled. "Just tell us!"

"Luke even said that he'd help me out with my work if I get stuck!" Lexie looked like she'd just had a weight the size of a baby elephant taken off her shoulders.

"Ah, that's sweet," Nisha smiled.

"So..." A huge grin split Lexie's face. "Are you all free next Saturday?"

"Yes!" Jas cheered. "I've been keeping it free. I never doubted for a second you'd get there!"

We giggled.

"Who else are you going to invite?" I asked as we headed to registration.

"Well, Mum and Dad said me and Luke could invite four friends each," Lexie explained. "But I can't think of anyone else I'd like there besides you three."

Lexie stopped. Aleisha was ahead of us at the lockers. She looked up briefly, before closing her locker and walking quickly away. Lexie acted like she hadn't noticed Aleisha as we headed to our form room.

Suddenly I heard running footsteps along the corridor behind me. I turned to see Ed. He slowed to a walk, grinning.

"I read your blog last night," he said to me. "It was brilliant. Thanks, Ellie."

I flushed scarlet. "Great," I mumbled, aware of my BFFs nudging each other beside me.

Play to Win

"Your picture was cool, too, Nisha," he added.

"Thanks, Ed," Nisha smiled. "Glad you liked it!"

Ed nodded. Then he quickly nipped past us through the door to registration.

I looked at my BFFs, who were all dissolving into giggles.

"What?" I asked, but I couldn't hide the pinkness in my cheeks, or keep the smile from my face. As we walked into the classroom, I turned the conversation back to Lexie's party, to take the attention off me.

Kirsty overheard us talking about it. "You're such a tomboy, Lexie," she sighed. "That sounds like my nightmare birthday party."

"Well, it's a good job you're not invited then, isn't it?" Lexie quipped happily.

Luckily Kirsty didn't have the chance to say anything else, because Miss Dubois came into the room and called for quiet. Then she announced to the whole class that, thanks to Lexie's idea, Mr Lawrence had agreed to hold a charity match day on the first Saturday of the Easter holidays. It would feature a match between the Year Seven boys' football team and the newly formed girls' team, plus a teachers versus students match, featuring the senior school football team. All proceeds would go to the skate park. Ed almost fell off his chair. He looked over, and gave Lexie a huge thumbs up.

"Now, there is lots of work to do in preparation," Miss Dubois continued, "but not much time. We're going to hold a Year Seven meeting on Monday at lunchtime."

On Saturday, I took my BFFs along with me to Ajay's house to watch the band rehearsing. They were set up in Ajay's garage. It wasn't exactly big, and it was pretty chilly in there. The car was parked outside on the drive while the drums, electric guitar, bass guitar and microphone were all set up inside, plugged in to a small PA speaker system. The band was made up of Ajay, Travis and Dev, plus a girl called Misty from Freethorpe, who was the lead singer. She had a bright pink streak in her fringe, which she told us had got her into trouble at school.

Ajay's mum got us all drinks while the band finished setting up. Then they started to play. Me and my BFFs were blown away – literally! It was so loud in that small space and it felt like my whole body was vibrating!

Play to Win

They played lots of songs we all knew, and it sounded great. Jas started dancing along crazily. She tugged at Lexie's arm, trying to get her dancing, too, but Lexie just smiled at her and shook her head, refusing to get up. I made notes for my blog and Nisha snapped away with her camera. After they'd played through about six songs, they stopped for a break and we all sat and chatted. I asked them questions and they talked about their plans for the band and how they'd got started. They'd been playing together for almost a year!

"Yeah," Travis said. "When we first started playing, we sounded pretty rough. It took us a while to get it together, and work out who was doing what. But we've been practising loads and I think we sound pretty good now!"

As the boys went back to their instruments to tune up, before playing a few more songs, Jas whispered, "What's up, Lexie?"

Lexie smiled. "Is it that obvious?"

"Er, yes!" Jas said.

"I was just thinking that I might have been a bit foolish," Lexie admitted, "about challenging the boys to a match. I mean, we really aren't experienced as a team and that friendly proved one thing – we need time to gel. And time's one thing we don't have. The match is on the first Saturday of the Easter holidays. That's two weeks today!"

"Well, there was one positive thing about that match, though," Nisha pointed out.

"What?" Lexie asked, looking doubtful.

"The team can't get much worse, can it?" Nisha smiled.

"If you really want the best team, Lex," I said, "you need Aleisha back on board."

"I was thinking exactly the same thing," Lexie admitted reluctantly.

"Aleisha Okeke?" Misty asked. "I know her! We were at primary school together. In fact, she lives round the corner from here."

"Really?" said Lexie, brightening. "Maybe I should go and talk to her about it. I feel really bad about how we left things…"

"Her house is literally two minutes away. She lives at number thirty-seven Ashfield Road. If you go left out of here, it's the first street you come to."

"Let's go there now!" Jas said decisively. "Then you can make it up with her and she'll be back in the team – job done. Agreed? Good."

Lexie smiled and nodded.

"Well, I've got tons here for my blog post, so let's go!" I said.

We said goodbye to the band and left them to continue with their practice. Now we had a new mission.

"Here's number thirty-seven," Jas announced.

It was Aleisha who opened the door. She looked totally shocked to see us all there.

"Hi," Lexie said with a small smile.

"Hey," Aleisha frowned, looking slightly suspicious. "What are you guys doing here?"

"Um, can we come in?" Jas asked. Aleisha stepped back into her neat hallway to let us past.

"Off to the left," Aleisha told us. We trooped into the living room.

"So?" Aleisha asked as she sat on the sofa. We all sat down, too. Lexie seemed suddenly reluctant to say anything. Nisha nudged her.

"Well, I wanted to ... to say sorry," Lexie finally blurted out. "About the football and wanting to be captain."

Aleisha seemed to relax a bit, but she waited to hear what else Lexie had to say.

"You'd have made a brilliant captain," Lexie continued a bit awkwardly. "And we've got this charity match coming up and I'd really love it if you came back on to the team for it. We'll be a laughing stock if we play badly and I … I think we've got a much better chance of winning if you play…"

Lexie trailed off. We all watched Aleisha, to see how she would react. For a second she was quiet, then she broke into an enormous, infectious grin.

"You know what," she said, "I shouldn't have just stomped off like that, so I'm sorry, too. I always wished there was a girls' football team at Priory Road and I guess I was a bit jealous that you'd done something about it. I really wanted to break the deadlock because I'm desperate to get back in the team. So, can we just forget all that stuff and get on with more important things?"

Lexie smiled and breathed a sigh of relief.

"I watched the home match," Aleisha went on. "I had a few ideas for getting the team to come together more. We need to practise short passes, not huge long ones that trickle into the opposition's path, or go out of play. Oh, and I think that we need more target practice. Zophia and you both had chances, but you didn't find the back of the net. What do you reckon?"

"Tell you what, why don't you come to mine now? Luke and Dad will be back from their football practice and we can have a kickaround in the garden. I've had a few ideas about how to improve, too."

"Great!" Aleisha stood up and we all followed her back into the hallway. "Then we can see whose ideas are best!" she said, pulling on her trainers.

Lexie was about to react, when she realized that Aleisha was teasing and grinned. Aleisha called out to her parents, to let them know where she was going, and we set off.

As we sat on the rumbling bus, Lexie glanced over to Aleisha. "I know it's short notice and everything," she said, "but are you free next weekend? It's my birthday – I'm going to The Adventure Forest."

Aleisha's face lit up. "I've been pestering Mum and Dad to let me go there for ages! I'd love to, thanks, Lexie – yes!"

We all grinned. Aleisha and Lexie had so much in common!

Back at Lexie's house, Lexie's dad, who was a coach

for the local youth team, made a few suggestions.

"We're never going to be ready in time!"

"For the charity match?" Mr Jones asked.

"You've got to get the rest of the team up to scratch, Lex," Luke chipped in. "If you don't, you'll just embarrass yourselves. Jordan will never let you live it down."

"Well, you can't back out now," Jas pointed out, "we've got a huge meeting about it on Monday – Mr Lawrence is involved, it's all official!"

Mr Jones looked at the girls. "I think I may have a solution..."

Birthday boy Luke has an Unlucky break...

"Your dad's going to offer extra coaching?" Georgie asked. It was the start of the meeting and Aleisha and Lexie had gathered the girls' team together quickly so that they could catch up without the boys wigging in.

"This Sunday, and then after school on Thursdays up until the match," Lexie said.

"That'll be on top of our Wednesday after school and Friday lunchtime practice with Mrs Townsend, so it'll be intense," Aleisha added, "but worth it if we want a chance in this match."

"I'm up for that," Zophia said. "Jordan will be unbearable if the boys beat us!"

All the girls nodded, and Lexie and Aleisha grinned.

"Now, everyone, this is a very exciting prospect for Priory Road," Mr Lawrence began. "The charity match day is sure to raise a lot of money for the skate park renovations if we organize it well. I hope that you'll all get behind it and be true team players. And that doesn't just mean the students who are representing their teams on the pitch. It includes those of you who might help design T-shirts for the players, drum up interest from local businesses for sponsorship or help sell tickets.

"Make sure you spread the word! We'd like to see lots of students and parents there, and any of your friends from other schools should come along, too. I'm sure they all can't wait for the chance to see me and your other teachers attempting to hold our own against this school's top football players. And this will also be the very first eleven-a-side match for our brand-new Year Seven girls' football team!"

Nemone put up her hand, looking excited.

"Yes, Nemone?" Mr Lawrence asked.

"Could we organize a cheerleading team, too?"

"Wonderful idea."

"This is going to be so exciting!" Kirsty said to Eliza.

Play to Win

"I think the girls' strip should be really pink and flowery. What do you think?"

"No way!" Lexie called out, overhearing her. "You two aren't wearing the strip, remember, the team is! And I'm not playing in front of loads of people in pink!"

"But it's a girls' team!" Kirsty pointed out. "I just thought that this would make a really clear statement about that!"

Lexie looked on the verge of wavering, surprised that Kirsty had such a good point.

"Maybe we could settle for purple?" Nisha suggested.

Eliza, Kirsty and Lexie looked at each other for a second, then nodded.

"That sounds OK," Lexie agreed. "Just."

Once that was settled, Jas, Lexie and I went over to join the group discussing sponsorship for the match.

"I think we should ask Joey from the Ace Diner," Jas said. "I know! If he agrees, the team could even be called the Diner-mites!"

"That's perfect!" I said. "I bet the team love it!"

"And I'll talk to the manager at Sports Mad, the big sports shop in town," Ed piped up. "They might be interested, as it's to help keep the skate park open."

"Good idea," said Miss Dubois. "We're looking for businesses to help us with publicity, and also to offer prizes for the raffle. That way, we'll be raising even more money for the skate park."

Lexie turned to us and grinned. "I can't believe this has turned into such a big deal!" she said. "It's so cool!"

It seemed that her challenge hadn't been such a bad idea, after all!

Saskia and Nemone organized cheerleading sessions, overseen by Miss Gill, a student PE teacher, on the playing fields at lunchtimes. I went out to watch, so that I could blog about it, and Nisha popped outside one lunchtime, too, to take some photos. The cheerleaders were practising their goal celebration, with Saskia and Nemone stepping up, then springing off the other girls' cupped hands against a bright blue, cloudless sky. They performed the splits mid-air, their purple pom-poms twinkling in the sun. Nisha clicked away rapidly, then immediately checked back on her photos in the viewfinder, an intense look on her face.

"What's up?" I asked, putting away my notepad and walking over to her.

Play to Win

"The cheerleaders!" She turned the camera to me so I could see what she was looking at, breaking out into a grin. Saskia and Nemone were both captured, at full splits, pom-poms fluffed up by their trainers, grinning as their long curly hair flew out sideways against the sun.

"That's an awesome pic!" I said, patting Nisha on the back.

"This is it! I think this will be perfect for the competition!" Nisha grinned.

With a week to go until the match, Mrs Townsend put up the team sheets. Wiggy was on the teachers' team and Mr Wood was playing, too, as well as Mr Flight, Miss Dubois and Miss Dunn – and Mr Lawrence and Terrifying Townsend herself, of course! They were going to be up against the main school football team, which was mostly made up of boys from Year Ten and Eleven.

There was a big crowd at the noticeboard. Luke had been up there, checking out the teams. When he spotted us, he smiled.

"So, Lex, we'll definitely be playing against each

other," he said, "we're both in the teams for the Year Seven match!"

"Then we'll really find out who's best!" Lexie grinned, elbowing him playfully. He smiled, shaking his head. Then Lexie got serious. "Did you see who's captain for the girls' team?" she asked, looking like she wasn't sure she wanted to know.

"Aleisha," Luke said, giving Lexie a small smile.

Aleisha appeared at that moment amongst the throng.

"Well done on making captain," Lexie said. "You deserve it."

"Thanks," Aleisha said, "but I don't reckon that the captain's always the best player, just so you know."

Jordan was in the crowd, too. He leaned over, grinning. "Let battle commence!"

After the week that we'd had, with all of us busy on our own projects, it felt like I'd hardly spent any time with my BFFs. The deadline for the Springtime photography competition was Monday morning, so Nisha had been going through all her photos over and over, trying to figure out which one to enter. I'd been busy with the blog. New writers were popping up each time I checked the intranet. And people had added comments to some of my posts, too! Jas had been spending every spare second preparing for her next performing arts class, juggling with whatever she could get her hands on. And Lexie was so focused on the training in preparation for the match that she couldn't talk about anything else. I couldn't wait to hang out with them all – literally! – at The Adventure Forest that weekend!

"Right, have we got everyone?" Mr Jones called out. There was a bunch of us all standing outside Lexie's front door, ready to set off on our Adventure Forest trip. We'd already been inside and given Lexie all her presents, leaving a pile of sparkly wrapping paper in the middle of the lounge. Me, Jas and Nisha had clubbed together to get her a new pair of shin pads, which she screamed and danced about with. She certainly seemed to like them. Aleisha gave her a pair of long football socks, and Lexie's parents had bought both her and Luke a new pair of football boots.

"OK, let's go!" Mr Jones sounded a bit frazzled already as he slid open the door to the hired minibus and all Lexie and Luke's friends piled in. The noise on the minibus got louder and louder as we shouted across to each other! Luke had invited his friends from the Year Seven football team, including Jordan, who spent the whole journey making comments about how the boys were going to thrash the girls.

"Just wait till we're on the pitch before you get too confident," Aleisha called back, craning round in her seat to look back at the boys. "You might just get a surprise!"

"The only way you'll win," Jordan replied with a smirk, "is if we're too busy laughing at your girly shots to score any goals."

I looked round at the chattering, laughing boys. I couldn't help wishing that Ed was among them. Before I could stop it, a little sigh slipped out.

"What's up?" Jas asked.

"Oh, nothing..." I said.

But Jas must have read my mind because she grinned massively. "Are you missing Ed? You are, aren't you!" she whispered, so no one else could hear.

I went pink. "Er, hardly...!" But I couldn't stop a smile spreading across my face at the mention of his name.

"Ahhhh! I knew it!" Jas giggled.

Play to Win

"What are you two laughing about?" Lexie asked, leaning forward between the gap in the seat. Jas looked at me and started to giggle again. I couldn't help joining in.

"Has everyone got a harness?" our instructor asked. "Everyone got a safety helmet?"

We all shouted back yes. We were in a little glade, with all the humungous trees towering above us. The instructor went through all the safety instructions and I felt myself start to shake – I wasn't quite sure whether it was the cold, excitement or nerves at the thought of the dizzying height.

Nisha must have noticed. "How's your ankle?" she asked, looking concerned. "Do you think you'll be OK?"

I realized that I'd hardly thought about it for a couple of days. I put all my weight on it for a second and there was only the slightest twinge. "It feels loads better," I smiled. Suddenly I felt a bit more up for the challenge ahead!

Then, we were off. The boys raced ahead, thankfully, so that we could just enjoy it without them making comments. Lexie and Aleisha were swinging between trees as if they'd been doing it since they were born.

I stood on the first platform, looking at the huge drop below me and feeling my knees quake, despite the fact that I was completely strapped in. I grabbed the ropes either side of me, then started to step out on to the first of a series of fixed platforms, squealing when I thought I was going to lose my balance. Luckily, I had the other girls for company! Nisha and Jas were as unsteady as I was. Jas was in her element, shrieking with excitement and giggling hysterically on the zipwire.

When we got to the last, terrifyingly long zipwire, I whizzed down it, screaming the whole way, before thudding to the ground! We gathered in a group at the bottom and made our way to the café. We were all talking over each other excitedly, about the near slips and falls we'd had, all of them hugely exaggerated now we were safely on the ground! Even Jordan had stopped annoying us for once, he was so busy telling everyone how he'd been the quickest and the most daring.

Once we'd finished our drinks, Lexie's parents rounded us up and we piled out of the café. We headed along the woodchip pathway to the car park.

Play to Win

Jordan was still monkeying around at the back of the group, pretending to climb the trees. He called out for the other boys to look. Luke was just ahead of us and he turned to see what Jordan was up to. He grinned, walking backwards for a couple of steps. As he turned back again he tripped on a tree root and went flying. He put out his arm as he crashed to the ground with a thud and let out an almighty cry. We all crowded round as Lexie rushed to his side, closely followed by their mum and dad.

His face was flushed, and it looked like he was trying really hard not to cry. A couple of instructors ran over and took him to the first-aid tent. The rest of us were ushered on to the minibus to wait. We chatted nervously until Luke reappeared, his arm in a sling. Everyone cheered.

"Are you OK?" Lexie asked anxiously.

"They think it might be broken," he winced. "I've got to go and have it X-rayed when we get home."

Nisha's officially talented and we have a secret to keep!

Luke was off school on Monday – the X-ray showed that he'd broken his right wrist.

"I am so jealous!" Lexie sighed.

"What, of his broken wrist?" Aleisha asked. "That's so wrong!"

"I know!" Lexie grinned. "But he's getting extra time off school, that's all!"

As it turned out, the last week of school was pretty fun. Nisha had finally decided on the photo she was going to enter in the competition – the one of the cheerleaders. She had even done some work on retouching it, using the tips she'd got from the

136

photography club. She raced to see Mrs Fox first thing on Monday morning and hand in her entry.

"When will you get the results?" I asked as Nisha came back into registration.

"This Friday," she grinned. "Last day of term!"

Tickets for the match were selling fast and the hype was growing by the day. The girls' team had an away match on Thursday, after school. Lexie's dad was going to swap his coaching session to the Wednesday evening, so that they didn't miss out. Lexie was so excited she could barely sit still!

And, finally, after hours of work, it was time to present our PSHE projects in class. Zac went before me – his presentation was about opening a tuck shop at school. It made everyone laugh, but all I could think about as he neared the end was having to give mine next!

"Go, Ellie," Lexie whispered as Zac walked back to his seat, "you can smash this!"

"Thanks, Lex," I whispered back. I made my way to the front of the classroom, my legs a bit jelly-like. My piece of paper with the speech on was shaking slightly in my hand, so I decided to lie it on the desk instead. I pretty much knew most of it off by heart, so it was only a prompt, but at least it gave me something other than a scary sea of faces to look at! I put my mocked-up newspaper on the desk, too, which I was going to pass round at the end.

"Whenever you're ready, Ellie," Mr Blaxhall said, from where he was standing near the back of the class.

I nodded, and cleared my throat. "This is a campaign to start a school newspaper," I began. "I wanted to have a place that was 'access all areas' for Priory Road students, where we got to have our own say, in our own way."

I risked a glimpse up from my speech. Everyone was listening. Jas beamed at me encouragingly. As I carried on speaking, my nerves began to dissolve. And, as I held up my newspaper and talked about some of the articles, then passed it round, my confidence surged.

Once I'd finished I felt a huge wave of relief. It hadn't been anywhere near as bad as I'd thought it might be, but I still couldn't wait to reach my seat, knowing it was over! Next was Lexie's turn. Her talk went down a storm, especially when she played the video.

As the bell went, and we all started to leave the room, Nisha suddenly piped up. "Oh, I meant to tell you who's asked for a ticket for the charity match," she said, turning to us with a broad smile.

"Who?" I asked.

"Poppy! She was planning to come and stay over Easter anyway, but she's going to come up on Friday evening now, so that she can see the game."

"Even though Luke's not playing?" Lexie asked.

Nisha nodded. "She wants to come and nurse the patient," she giggled.

On the day of the girls' next match, Jordan's jibes reached new levels.

"I hope this match isn't as embarrassing as the last one," he said smugly. "Although you'll have to get used to losing for when we smash you on Saturday."

The girls had become expert at ignoring the boys' digs, but as they got ready to head off for the match, it was clear that they were all nervous. Nisha, Jas and I gave Lexie a hug.

"Good luck!" we chorused.

"And text us as soon as you finish!" I added.

Lexie smiled. "Thanks! Keep your fingers crossed – we're going to need it."

By eight o'clock that evening I still hadn't heard anything. I was so impatient to find out the result of the match that I decided not to wait any longer. I texted her.

So??!

Sshhhhhh, will tell u tomoz – secret! x

The next morning, we collared Lexie at the lockers.

"How did it go?" Nisha asked.

Lexie broke into a huge grin, then pulled us to one side. "Listen, you have to keep this really, really quiet."

The three of us nodded.

"We won!" Lexie whispered. "Three–two!"

"Wow! That's gre—" Jas cried. Lexie grabbed her mid-sentence.

"Sssh!" she said, looking round quickly to check no one was listening. "The boys aren't allowed to know! We've decided to tell them that we lost – that way Jordan and his gang will expect us to be terrible tomorrow."

We got to the classroom for registration and Jordan

was leaning back in his chair, gloating. "Heard about the match," he said. "Seven–nil. That's almost worse than last time!"

"Give them a chance!" Trin said, leaping to the team's defence. "They've only just got together."

"Exactly," Maisie agreed. "We're not going to be amazing straight away."

"OK, OK!" Jordan grinned, holding up his hands. "But I still reckon they better be prepared for an even bigger defeat tomorrow, that's all!"

There was a real end-of-term spirit all day. At lunchtime we rushed with Nisha to the Social noticeboard. Mrs Fox was just pinning up the results of the photography competition.

She stood back as people started to gather round.

"Wow! I got Highly Commended!" Nisha said, turning to us.

"Well done," Mrs Fox said. "I thought your composition was original. You've got natural talent, Nisha. I'm especially impressed with your work, given that you've only just started at the club. I think photography's something you could really excel at. You'll be coming back again next term, I hope?"

"Absolutely!" Nisha said, beaming. "I love it!"

"Good good," Mrs Fox nodded. "I'll see you then."

We all hugged Nisha and congratulated her. She was beaming with pride.

"Now that Nisha's done such a brilliant job in the photography competition," I said, "it's just down to you and the team, Lexie, to show the boys what you can do!"

Lexie grinned. "The match last night was great, so we're ready to give it a shot. I can't wait!"

Demba Keshi got it right!

"Poppy! Nisha!" Jas called out.

The girls spotted us and ran over.

"Who ever thought I'd walk back through those gates so soon!" Poppy laughed, her green eyes twinkling. She was looking as cool as ever, in her black biker jacket, leggings and biker boots. She had a little cream beanie on and, under her jacket, a purple football shirt.

"How did you get your hands on that?!" Jas gasped, pointing at the team shirt that Poppy was wearing.

"Friends in the right places," Poppy grinned,

winking at Nisha. I noticed her glance round.

"I haven't seen him yet," I smiled, knowing exactly who she was looking for! "Although Lexie's here, so your boyfriend must be, too, somewhere!"

At that moment we heard a shout. Lexie was sprinting towards us, her face a picture of excitement.

"So good to see you again!" She hugged Poppy. "Are you ready to watch a 'Diner-mite' performance?"

"It better be that good," Poppy grinned back. "I haven't come all this way to see you guys get whitewashed!"

"Well, we'll find out soon enough," Lexie grinned nervously. "I've got to go and get changed. See you later!"

"Good luck, Lexie!" we all chorused. She turned and ran off.

"I'm nervous for them!" I whispered.

"Oooh, look, there's Luke!" Nisha pointed out. He came towards us through the crowd, looking a bit awkward. His arm was in a blue plaster cast from just below his elbow.

"Hi," he said shyly.

"Hey!" Poppy smiled. "Can I sign that?" she asked, nodding towards his arm.

Play to Win

Luke grinned. "I brought a marker pen!"

We walked over to the pitch, so we could get a good view, and waited for the first match to begin. I couldn't believe how many people there were.

"We must have raised loads of money," Nisha whispered to me.

"Oooh, it's about to start!" Jas nudged us. The cheerleaders, led by Saskia and Nemone, ran on to the pitch and the crowd began to whistle, cheer and clap. They took up their positions along one side.

Next the boys' team ran out on to the pitch with Mr Lawrence. Nisha took out her camera and started to snap away. Jordan put the ball he was carrying down in the centre of the pitch and the boys began to pass it between themselves. Then Mrs Townsend led the girls' team out and they began to warm up, too.

Eventually Mr Lawrence called, "Teams, you have two minutes!"

Terrifying Townsend called the girls over to her for final instructions.

As they walked to their positions on the pitch, Jordan laughed. "Say goodbye to dignity and hello to defeat."

Zophia and the girls smiled at each other, like they

didn't really care, then Lexie gathered them into a huddle.

"Look, Diner-mites, we may not be favourites to win this match," she said firmly, "and the boys may expect us to fail, but that doesn't mean we have to. It's time to show everyone how much hard work we've put into this team, and how much we believe in it. We're playing to win! Let's go!"

Aleisha lost the toss and the boys got to kick off. For a second a hush fell over the crowd. Then the whistle blasted shrilly and they were off. Lexie rushed forward and deftly whipped the ball from Jordan's feet and set off up the field.

"He was so not expecting that!" Nisha screamed. "Come on, Lexie!"

Tom charged towards her and Maisie shouted out, "To me!"

Lexie looked up and struck the ball, sending it forward just as Tom barged into her, almost knocking her to the ground. One thing was certain – this was going to be a full-force match. Maisie passed to Zophia, the girls' striker, but Max intercepted it and booted it back up the other end of the pitch. Lexie and Georgie chased it, but Jamie outran them and picked it up. He turned with the ball and tapped it sideways to Mica, who blasted it towards goal. Sammy didn't stand a chance and it smacked into the back of the net. The cheerleaders went into one of their routines, jumping up and touching their toes with their pom-poms. Mr Lawrence blew his whistle. Lexie grabbed the ball and raced back to the centre circle. She kept her cool, but she didn't want to waste a second.

"Come on, Diner-mites!" I yelled.

Only minutes later, the boys swept through the girls' defence. Jamie deftly tapped the ball past Sammy, who got a gloved fingertip on it, but not enough to deflect it from goal. Two–nil. I felt tight in my stomach, just imagining how Lexie would be feeling right now. But her face was a mask of steely determination. None of them were about to admit defeat and after the ball had been passed up and down the pitch a few times, Georgie intercepted it and passed it decisively to Lexie, who kicked it to Aleisha with one touch. Almost instinctively, Aleisha turned and as she tried to shoot, Max dived and headed it out of play.

"Corner!" Mr Lawrence shouted.

Lexie got the team organized into one of the formations her dad had taught them. She walloped the ball, and sent it curving straight into Aleisha's path. The captain launched in, pushing past the boys who tried to block her, and slammed it into the back of the net with her right foot. The girls all ran to each other, high-fiving.

"Two—one!" Nisha yelled, just as the cheerleaders burst into life again with their routine.

A second later the whistle for half-time blew. Both teams looked grateful for the break. But it wasn't long before they were back on the pitch.

"Come on, Lexie!" Jas screamed. "Come on, the Diner-mites!"

Lexie made a sliding tackle against Jordan, just tipping the ball, and before he knew what had happened she was back on her feet and racing up the pitch, dribbling past Tom, then Damon, until she heard Maisie shout and quickly passed it. Maisie turned and slotted the ball past Darren into the goal. The cheerleaders and the crowd went wild.

"Two—all — why can't they stop now?!" I asked, feeling all tense. Finally the boys got their revenge. Tom walloped the ball and it sailed past Sammy, to a mixture of groans and cheers from the crowd. Sammy collected the ball from the back of the net, looking apologetic.

Play to Win

"The girls can't win now, can they?" Poppy sighed, looking distraught as she stood there, squeezing Luke's hand.

"It's not over till the whistle blows," Luke said. He was looking as tense as the rest of us. It seemed impossible for the Diner-mites to win – there was only a minute left to play and the score was 3–2 to the boys. Jordan made another killer run down the left side. Luke jumped about like he was living every move on the pitch. I suddenly realized that he was cheering for Lexie and the girls, not Jordan!

"Tackle him, Lexie!" he shouted. Lexie ran at an angle, reaching Jordan as he approached the goal. She stretched out her foot, flicking the ball away from Jordan. By the time Jordan went to follow the ball, Lexie had already trapped it and back-heeled it to Holly. Holly collected it, but as Mica closed in she passed it back to Lexie, who charged off up the pitch to a roar from the crowd.

Lexie put her head down and flew like the wind; when she saw Tom heading her way, she spun past him. The goal was looming, but Aleisha was calling on the other side. Lexie hesitated for a second, then sidekicked the ball to Aleisha, who hammered it towards the goal. The crowd half-cheered, but it was too soon – the ball hit the post and rebounded. But suddenly Zophia launched herself at the loose ball, and with a determined scream she headed the ball towards goal. It wasn't a powerful shot, but Darren couldn't reach it and it sailed into the back of the net. The crowd erupted. Me and Jas turned to each other and leaped up and down.

A second later the whistle blew and Jordan stomped over to the rest of the team.

"Three–all," Aleisha laughed as they left the pitch together. "Not quite the whitewash you were predicting, right?"

Jordan scowled. But the other boys clapped the result graciously.

The teams stayed out, pulling on hoodies and tracksuit bottoms over their kits, to see the teachers versus students match. Lexie made her way over through the crowd and got swamped by Poppy, Luke, her three BFFs and her mum and dad.

"Three–all!" her dad kept saying. "Three–all! Can you believe it?!"

"Yes, Dad. Now let me watch the match!" she laughed. She looked the happiest she had all term.

Play to Win

The next match was full of light-hearted pantomime booing and cheering, especially when Mr Wood or Wiggy got the ball, or Daniel, our head boy.

The game ended in a defeat for the teachers, which they all took in good humour. Miss Dubois still looked as immaculate and mud-free as she had at the start!

When the match finished, Mrs Townsend marched to the centre of the pitch with Mr Lawrence and blew her whistle so loudly that everyone fell silent.

"Before everyone goes, I've got a couple of announcements," she yelled. "Thank you for making this a very enjoyable day – hopefully it will have raised lots of money towards making the skate park safe again."

A cheer went up from the crowd, then she carried on. "The Priory Road Year Seven girls' team have played brilliantly, and their commitment has been impressive. From next term there will be a permanent girls' team."

Luke gave Lexie a thumbs up from his good hand as Lexie grinned.

"Looks like Demba Keshi got it right," Jas laughed.

"And one final announcement," Mr Lawrence added, raising his voice over the murmuring crowd.

"Player of the match for the Year Sevens goes to the person who assisted in each of their sides' three goals." There was a dramatic pause. "Lexie Jones!"

"What? Me?" Lexie gulped, looking genuinely shocked.

"Yes – you! Get up there!" Aleisha beamed, pushing her forward. Lexie jogged on to the pitch and proudly collected a little medal to a huge cheer. We whooped and jumped with delight.

After the announcements were finished we headed into town along with the rest of the girls' team and the cheerleaders. We made straight for the only possible after-match celebration hang out – the Ace Diner!

Joey's face lit up when the purple-shirted team spilled in. "Free shakes all round!" he yelled out when he heard the score.

Not long after, the boys' team appeared, along with Luke and Poppy and a few others from the crowd. I looked round, but I couldn't see any sign of Ed and my heart dropped, just a bit.

"Oooh, look!" Nisha squealed. "Look who Josh is talking to!"

Play to Win

We all craned our necks and saw that he was in deep conversation with Aleisha.

"Quick, let's listen!" Jas whispered. But as we eavesdropped, we soon realized that all they were talking about was football.

"Well, I think we should raise a toast," I said, holding my glass aloft. "To success!"

We all chinked glasses and cheered.

"Can you believe it's coming up to our last term of Year Seven at Priory Road?" I said to my BFFs as we sat happily slurping our shakes.

Lexie shook her head. "It's gone so quickly!"

At the start of the year I was too afraid to say boo to a goose, so who would have thought that by Easter I'd have performed in a talent show, helped out in the Christmas production, tried playing football and written my own blog.

"Guys, what do you think about this idea for my final blog this half term?" I asked.

"What?" Jas asked as my BFFs turned to me.

"Well, I've written loads about what's been going on this term, but what if I wrote about what it's like to start Year Seven?" I said. "Then any Year Sixes who are thinking of coming to Priory Road could read it.

It might make them feel less worried about the whole thing!"

"The newbies will be coming to have a look round the school soon," Nisha pointed out. "Just like we did months ago. I think that's a fab idea."

"Just think," Jas grinned. "We won't be the newbies for much longer!"

"So," I said, getting out my notepad and pen. "What are your top tips?"

"Tip number one," Jas said as I began to scribble them down. "Don't fall out with your best mate! They'll be your biggest support."

"Number two," Nisha continued, smiling as Aleisha waved over to us. "Make lots of new BFFs – you don't just need to have one!"

"Three," Lexie chipped in. "Don't be afraid to try lots of new things!"

I didn't even notice Ed come in as I was writing all the tips down in my notebook. Then, all of a sudden, he appeared at our table. That was my fourth tip. If a guy plays the fool, give him a chance. He might just turn out to be nice...

Only I didn't write that one down!

Have you read?

New year, new term and it's
great to be **BACK TOGETHER** with my
BFFs after the Christmas hols! But Nisha's
step-sister Poppy has come to stay and
she's **NOT** happy to be here.

It seems that **SUPER-COOL** Poppy will do
anything to **MESS THINGS UP** for Nisha.

*It looks like Nisha is heading
for a total freak-out!*

Also Available: